£2.49

at /1/3

Taking Scarlet
as a Real Colour

Taking Scarlet as a Real Colour

◆

Evelyn Conlon

THE
BLACKSTAFF
PRESS

BELFAST

• A BLACKSTAFF PAPERBACK ORIGINAL •

Blackstaff Paperback Originals present new writing, previously
unpublished in Britain and Ireland, at an affordable price.

First published in 1993 by
The Blackstaff Press Limited
3 Galway Park, Dundonald, Belfast BT16 0AN, Northern Ireland
with the assistance of
The Arts Council of Northern Ireland

© Evelyn Conlon, 1993
All rights reserved

Typeset by Paragon Typesetters, Queensferry, Clwyd

Printed by The Guernsey Press Company Limited

A catalogue record for this book
is available from the British Library

ISBN 0-85640-501-9

ACKNOWLEDGEMENTS

Some of these stories have already been published in *Wildish Things* (Attic Press), *Fiction International*, *God* (Serpent's Tail), the *Sunday Tribune*, and the *Journal of Irish Literature*.

My thanks to Tara, for information, to Teresa, for practical help, to Sally and Helen, for friendship and books given during a dodgy few years, and to Gina for her line.
To Fintan, as always, for everything.

with much love
and thanks
to Warren and Trevor

CONTENTS

THE UNDEATHING OF GERTRUDE

There was Betty, a face so fragile it might disappear before you as if it hadn't been coloured in. And Tim, he could wipe that sorrowful look off his face, he would get a woman – old men might say more fool she, surely no one could marry that cheap, and they would know that what she was marrying him for wouldn't last – still he would get a woman. And Mary, ragged-looking as a crooked road, always pretending to think about one of her children, but that was bluffing, she couldn't bear to think of her mother and father, that's why she wore her maternal look. And James, home from America, twitching to get back to his plastic life, where to own was to understand. Well, it's good that Gertrude hadn't died after all.

The children hung around for a few days, generally getting on his nerves as they swayed about the place, having long telephone conversations with their friends, explaining over and over again how their mother had died and her not dead at all. When they left, he and Gertrude sighed with relief.

Eddie McGivern got thin gradually. He had to be careful, you see, because his neighbours, as well as his children, believed that his wife was dead, so he was forced to buy food for only one and then share it with Gertrude. As she had always been a very healthy eater, this meant that even less than half of what he bought went into his own mouth.

The shopkeeper in the village told the next-door neighbour, as they discussed him in doubtful voices, that he seemed to be doing grand, he hadn't lost his appetite or anything like that judging by his purchases. Still, he was getting thin and no doubt about it. The neighbour said, yes, indeed, he could vouch for the appetite because he had called many mornings and he was having two boiled eggs for his breakfast, two, that was a thing he could never do himself, have more than one boiled egg.

The mornings the neighbour called were indeed the days on which Eddie and Gertrude had boiled eggs – the unfortunate thing was that Eddie could have an egg only one half the number of times, because that shopkeeper was so nosy she would twig that there was something up if he was still buying the same amount of eggs that they had always bought before people said that Gertrude had died. The same with bread, butter, milk, bacon, everything in fact.

Eddie McGivern was a different kind of man. When he first met Gertrude he brought her out for meals occasionally, which was not normal at the time – people ate in those days, they didn't talk about food – and asked her how was that and was the dessert nice. They went for long walks, both of them very interested in scenery. They exhausted themselves describing it to each other, taking private pleasure out of what their descriptions actually meant, look at that hollow in the tree, you can put your hand in it; this valley is always wet. Perhaps they were before their time. Eddie knew people who had to beg guests to come to their wedding. Not Gertrude. People wanted to visit them even years after they got married. Gertrude was a navigator –

when she didn't know things, she felt them; he was a born pilot – he wasn't afraid to start anything. As they got older they didn't always finish their own sentences – sometimes they finished them for each other, sometimes they didn't bother. They lived together so long it was not a matter any more of love or hate. Of course, they hated each other sometimes, as is right for mature people. They still, even after people supposed her dead, had rows, naturally. On the days when he had a row with Gertrude he got into very bad form, really bad form. He knew that the neighbour noticed these moods but he never told him what caused them.

The summer after people said that Gertrude died, James came home from America. All the children came down and insisted on visiting the family grave. Eddie had a bit of an argument with Gertrude that morning because she said that for their sakes he should go, it would keep them happy, and he didn't see why he should have to, he hated graveyards. In the end she won. So there he was, caught among all these graves. No matter which way he turned they were there, rushing towards him like a bush fire. The children had put a railing around the grave as if someone was trying to get out. Well, if they were, the children were putting a stop to it. They had also put grotesque toys on top of it, plastic flowers and the like. Tim wandered around the graveyard reading aloud ancient headstones, he liked visiting old things. Pity, then, he didn't come home a bit more often, you'd think for his mother's sake he could try.

The children thought that Eddie was not coping well, he was distant and sometimes lapsed into conversation with himself, he was also getting very thin. They needled him so much about sitting around the place twiddling his thumbs that he decided that he would soon show them. Next week.

Eddie cleared out the old garage and put a door on it. He had to put the door on in order to stop the neighbours from seeing what he was doing. He drove to Dundalk where he bought all he needed. Then he set to showing the children just how busy he could make himself. He would paint Gertrude's and his life right up to this day. The board was twenty feet long and three feet deep, so there should be enough room. He pencilled in the important dates first, making sure to leave the right amount of space between them. He hammered on or stuck on symbols, mainly to use up space and to save him painting the entire board. He was not, after all, a real painter, so he needed guidelines as well as secret reminders. He put a sprig of hawthorn bush in the year they had built the house, hawthorn because it was steady. He put a piece of candle at the end of each year, that was for soft lights at Christmas and love so unbearable at times it might explode but it didn't, it just seeped out in touches and small things done for each other. They lit a candle in the window every Christmas Eve night before they left for midnight mass and pulled the curtains well back so they wouldn't catch fire. When they got electricity they simply switched on the lights. The light, first Christmas, because Gertrude thought one light in the kitchen was enough, they would not need bulbs in the bedrooms, but she changed her mind six months later. In the morning at early mass the frost sparkled like diamonds in the ground, the squeal of the bagpipe band starting up sent shivers down their backs.

4

He began at the top left-hand corner, painting a small boy and girl. The boy had his finger in his mouth more from contemplation than from fear, because he didn't know yet that there were things to fear. The girl was in her grandmother's house. After debts had been satisfied she was finally housed in an outhouse that had been a stable for stallions. The children thought it great fun until they discovered that they were going to live there. For real. The girl had her finger in her mouth but it meant a different thing. It was a pity that her children hated her, considering all this.

Eddie painted Gertrude at points in her life, he painted her every six inches or so, sometimes three inches from the top of the board, sometimes sitting, sometimes bending, sometimes at an angle. He painted her from above, climbed a ladder and painted her from her feet upwards, concentrating on her arms flung up, which looked different from there than if he had been standing in front of her. It was as if he was on a balcony watching a dancer down below. Gertrude was a great dancer.

As her years and the painting progressed she grew fatter and more comfortable. In dreams he painted himself beside her. Their bodies ran into each other in circles, head to toe, toe to head, head to toe, on and on into infinity like a hula hoop. They looked sometimes too like musical notes. There were moments when his portrait stood back from hers, baffled. When she was having babies, when she was feeding babies, when she was sick with exhaustion, when she was plain sick, the only thing he could do for her was to think about her and that's a fact. He couldn't talk to her or mind her, he could only think of her. He explained this in letters to her. He was writing letters to her now, asking her questions about little things that he couldn't remember. He was writing to her for two reasons: first, because she sometimes went away these days and was hard to contact, and second, it was easier to get all the questions down in a letter. He explained why he could only think of her, not mind her, when she was sick, why he had to occasionally drop out of their lives together, in case he learned too much. He told her that when she had first loved him he had walked around dazed – how could she love him? He told her that loving her had purified him.

Eddie had difficulty with colours. He had thought it would be so easy. His brushes were no good either. Earlier, the rasping of the jagged edge of his big brush had been the right sound and had made the right marks. But that was during the rough work – he had even used Gertrude's old turkey wing, her soot brush, then. He had used it to scratch the paint between the trees, to make them less dense because it was not true that they couldn't see out through them in the summertime. Light changes always got to their back door. The trees were hard though. They nearly sent him demented. He had to go out to them again and again to watch them, to take them in, because he couldn't paint outside. The neighbours. Just as well, the weather would never have held up.

Eddie was also having difficulty getting the depth, not the depth, but how deep it was, how far back, how far in, he could see it when he looked at it face-on, but it wasn't coming out right. This would not have hurt so much if he had not known the depth. He would take a break, go visit Mary, buy new brushes. In Dublin they might know something about how to mix colours.

Mary was all tense, like a top ready for spinning. How she could have got like that he couldn't imagine. He remembered trying to get her to say *ant* instead of *pismire* but no, she was too full of life for that. Mary was determined not to be dragged down by what must be interminable grief, her parents had got on so well, she couldn't bear to think about it. Although how anyone could have got on so well with either of them she didn't know. Still, he seemed remarkably well, mentally, not physically. Like Betty. She used 'in June' for shorthand instead of saying 'when mother died', or else she said 'that time mother died' as if it had been a once off thing and had not stayed happened.

Eddie talked and talked as if words were worth nothing. Mary scrubbed and scrubbed, so she might not hear them all. Eddie remembered the evening he gave her the paper with Campbell's auction in it, when she was a child: 'Read that out till we hear how good you are.' She read, 'A large farmhouse with water nearby and a lot of nice ties.' 'Niceties,' Eddie corrected her. She smiled, always pleasant while taking correction, not like the others. Gertrude beamed at them. Gertrude had furrows around her eyes from all the beaming she did.

Now Mary was scrubbing wildly to shut out the sound of his voice. She was afraid it would steal away her next decade or two and she hadn't got decades to play with. When he tried to link her for help crossing the busy roads, her arm froze as if he was attacking her. But Eddie had told

7

her that it was all right to believe that snow is blue. 'It looks blue, I can see,' he said, 'something to do with the light.' He had told her that the stars were lamps in the sky to guide us and that clusters of stars were countries in the sky. She scrubbed harder and harder.

Eddie and Mary walked out to the shops in Donnybrook.

'That's the house they cut in half to widen the road, isn't it?' he said.

Mary said, 'Yes', sharply.

'Imagine, their kitchen would have been here,' he tapped his foot on the path.

Mary sighed and hurried him on. She thought that herself every time she passed the house, but she couldn't afford to let him in on her life. If he had someone at home, that would be different. She was beginning to perspire heavily. He wanted to buy socks. She, for no reason, bought a pair of satin knickers with imitation pearls on them. If she hadn't bought them she might have been sucked in by him. The side of the knickers were cut out and the pearls were sewn around the edges in a triangle where the pubic hair would be. She would never wear them. Still, it didn't matter, it had put him in his place for a while, shut him up. Eddie thought that if she was buying stuff like that, maybe she wasn't as far gone as he had imagined. Mary left him in the hardware shop. He insisted that she go on home, he would be back in half an hour.

Mary's youngest said, 'That's the pits.'

'Do you know what that means?' Eddie asked.

'It means awful,' the child said.

'When the children in the workhouses had to dig their

own graves in the very flower beds they had planted, there were so many graves the flower beds had to be used too, that was called digging the pits. I think.'

Mary swung around. 'There's no need to frighten the child.'

'I didn't mean . . .'

In bed that night Mary said to her husband, 'My father showed me the sun dancing at the top of the ploughed field every Easter Sunday. He held a mirror to the light and showed me the sun dancing. I believed him. It was the reflection of bits of broken glass in the mirror but it doesn't matter. It was lovely believing him. Do you know that he told us that Jesus got away?' She finally went to sleep, determined to be gentler with her father but knowing that she wouldn't succeed.

Eddie went home, the hollow bit in the middle of him feeling bigger. He looked at his painting. He knew what he wanted it to be but he couldn't get it there. No matter how he pushed and cajoled, it didn't show. The Last Day, he had it pencilled in, Gertrude and he were there together. He hoped the Last Day didn't start too early, because Gertrude was never good in the mornings. The two of them hoped that all the neighbours would not be there. A person should be able to see that hope on their faces. But how could he, who was not a painter, paint a life? He was as exhausted as too-light rain trying to fill a bucket.

The auctioneer wrung his hands and told Mary that there was nothing he could have done about it. Eddie had come to him and asked that the contents of the house be sold. Only the contents. The neighbours turned up either to buy, to stand beside him in this sad hour, or to nose about. Some of them would have been wondering about the house. The first three items were sold (the auctioneer said he knew who had them and they were willing to give them back), when Eddie started to bid himself. It was a delph ornament, a bird that once had a clock in it. Eddie said to Seamus Patterson beside him that it belonged to Gertrude and that she had told him to buy it back for her. Painters often did that, he said, went to auctions and bought back their own paintings. He bid on every second item, the neighbours bid against him all right because it would have looked odd if they hadn't. Her father had signed a cheque, he had it right here, he hadn't cashed it, naturally. Her father hadn't taken the purchases with him either, just left and hasn't been seen since.

Mary thought the saddest part was the painting. She thought the bits that were finished were good and by the look of the pencilled scenes he knew what he was doing. Betty and Tim were devastated. They searched the roads and odd little lanes months after everyone else had given up. In the end they concentrated only on the roads between Ballintra and Dundalk. He had definitely been there recently according to the paint receipts. People think that these roads are going somewhere, that they are even a chart and mean something. This is not true. They're just an absolute mess of pointless lanes going nowhere, just there to confuse people who have lost one or both of their parents. Poor Betty, poor Tim. Betty hears voices at night talking to each other. James didn't come home because there wasn't much point, was there?

At night Mary tells her children that Jesus got away.

BEATRICE

Maybe it was the day that had caused it. A warm, over-generous June day, fifteen hours. The sky had been full of sun. The sort of day you are afraid to commit to memory in case it cracks if you stare. Beatrice Sherry had spent it being unbearably happy for no reason at all, well, that is if you think fresh air so tasty it can be swallowed and such sun, such sun, no reason at all.

All these days now she thought about what it might have been that caused it and how it happened. It was easier that way, blaming or thanking some vague it. Surely no one would expect her to say that she had done it herself, had landed herself here. Ah, but she had. She had stood beside him deliberately at the end of the party, they had been introduced casually as happens at aimless holiday parties flung together at the end of holiday nights in the west of Ireland. She found herself beside him, oh yes, found herself, then a waltz came on, I don't waltz, he said, I'll teach you, she said, and when she moved closer to get into the dance posi-tion a warm shiver like a needle went up between her legs and whistled to her head, making her feel faint. There was blood everywhere carousing, carousing through her veins. She didn't teach him to waltz, and next thing they found themselves at the door, ah yes, found themselves, he sup-posedly going – it would be easier to test the thing now – she supposedly staying. She held the door open for him, as if it was her house, which it wasn't; they each moved about one-eighth of one inch closer to the other, just enough to ensure that they could not then draw back. And no one knew whose tongue was drinking whose. They found themselves in his place (at least, he had a key) and they stripped each other slowly, rubbing their bare skin together, their tongues resting inside each other's mouths, or sucking ferociously, or gently licking. Her breasts felt sharp and brazen against him, she lowered her mouth and kissed and gently pulled his nipples. They hardened so readily he was shocked. They touched as much as they could stand, held each other's faces in their hands, and then pulled the breath from each other in one ecstatic coming that left them near tears and bewildered. They couldn't bear to take their arms from around their bodies.

But morning had to come. They slipped away – he to work, she to more holiday – afraid to say a word. She was terrified.

(It's not that she minded having an affair – she never liked that word, it was more like cold curry than what it was supposed to be – no one minds having an affair. Mind you, the one she'd had, five years ago, was just that, cold curry. I suppose you'd call it an affair, she met him twice, the time she met him and once more. The time she met him she was a bit drunk and she thought that he was the loveliest looking man since . . . since . . . God forgive her, she had it off with him in the car, well, there was nowhere else to go and anyway, she'd never done that before, even though she was nearly thirty-one. Maybe most people never did? They even went to the trouble of taking all their clothes off, except for

12

their socks. That trouble, that attention to the detail of each other's bodies, convinced her the next day that he was worth meeting again. It never struck her, or she forgot, that it was she who had insisted on all their clothes coming off. She also forgot how he kissed, which she thought was a bad sign, but still, you can't remember everything.

Between that night and the second time, a number of things were done. First there was the phone call, a few letters, and then the countdown. She had written him a letter telling him that she could meet him. Just to be sure of his flight – she didn't want to arrive at the wrong time and waste an hour or, more important, spend an hour looking so conspicuous that someone would be bound to notice her. A friend of hers was caught at the airport once; mind you, the woman who caught her was on her way back from a secret abortion in London so she could hardly talk – still, she enclosed an envelope addressed by herself to herself.

Although his other letters and postcards had always got through between the gas bills and the flat circulars, it would be foolish to risk getting caught at this late stage, hence the self-addressed envelope. Noticed by whom? Caught by whom? A husband of course. It wouldn't have been an affair without a husband. Yes, she had a husband, not a very good one, not a very exciting one, but a husband. (She was younger then and less cautious about husbands.)

She had read his, not the husband's, letters again before writing the arrangements to him. They had varied, she looked for signs of intelligence in them, once he had used the word 'generic' in an odd way and she had had to look it up in the dictionary, she wasn't quite sure if you could use it that way. You could, that was a good sign. In other letters he wrote about boring things, work and the like – he couldn't seriously believe that she was interested in the engineering possibilities of bridges over the M1 – but she supposed he wanted to fill up the page until he could get down to the real part of the letter, it was only decent to do that. The real parts of his letters always began with 'Well Beatrice'. Then he would reminisce about how they had met. She just had to read the 'Well Beatrice' bit and she'd lose her head altogether. She'd remember how they looked into each other's eyes as they came together in the car, which was hard to do and also brave of them really because you'd never know what you'd see in someone's eyes at a time like that. And then she'd remember the texture of his skin which was extraordinary, silky, like a precious memory from somewhere. Anyway, no need to go over all that again, he was on his way here for the weekend. She had felt a little obscene including the SAE without the stamp, an Irish stamp would be no good in England – an AE I suppose you'd call it. It was very premeditated, you couldn't explain it away by saying, I don't know what came over me. After his reply the countdown began.

DAY 5   Woke having had very bad dreams. Neck of nightdress soaking wet. Oh God, am I coming down with flu? By ten o'clock was all right so knew it was just guilt. The dream had been awful though. By twelve was normal again.
DAY 4   Had a terrible row with husband which I let get out of hand probably so I could say, see! he deserves me to go and have an affair.

DAY 3   Went into a panic about what I will do about car. It would be better to hire one so no one could recognise the number. Is licence in date?
DAY 2   Husband announces he is going away. With car. God I love him he's so good. I now have peace to book a hotel and hire a car.
DAY 1   Came out of car-hire place puce in the face . . . You'd think I wanted it for I don't know what, a bank robbery or worse.

She met him, by now mortified really, and doubtful that this was going to be worth the trouble. There were real people at the airport waiting for genuine reasons. There was a father hugging his son, his face trembling, and his daughter-in-law. Ah, his daughter-in-law, he squeezed her to him and let his face collapse. She had taken his lovely son but he couldn't blame her for that. How he loved that daughter-in-law. But no, they wouldn't stay at home. His wife was dead.

Beatrice recognised the engineer and immediately thought, I need a drink. They had a pint of Guinness and three cigarettes each. She hadn't been able to eat earlier so this was her breakfast. She drove to the hotel half drunk and amused at herself by now. At the first red light she leaned over and ran her lips over his face. Might as well. He kissed back and then she remembered. Surely things would be all right. Surely they would be worth it. But she had forgotten again how he kissed by the time they reached the hotel.

They had sex and he fell asleep – honest to God. Actually that was only passable, she had much better at home, she

15

decided. If he had stayed awake she mightn't have had time to think that. His skin wasn't soft at all. She listened to a woman next door torturing her child: 'Why do you make my life such a misery? I might stop being your mother, I might just do that, or you might give me a heart attack and how would you do then? With no mother.' Really she should get up and ring the ISPCC. Wimbledon was vaguely on the television. But she fell asleep too.

Later they went for a walk. And that was when the real trouble started. The man said some pointless thing. And that was as adventurous as he got with his words. She liked words, things to remember. Maybe if she gave him a pen and paper and asked him to write a letter? It would at least pass some of the time. One hour had gone by and he'd only said a thing or two, both of them about engineering. Jesus, please, I'll learn to pray again if you give this man a few words to say. You think three hours is a short time? Well, if you're doing nothing and saying nothing, it's one hundred and eight thousand seconds, or so it seems. She made some terrible excuse and escaped to her own home.

That had been the death of some small emotional insurance. Beatrice left his letters where they were for a few months because she was afraid to find out that she should have known. One night she took them out and skimmed over them quickly. They were sometimes like school essays, 'Christmas is a busy time', but then they could be surprising with the sureness of an entitled life lived. As she burned them she tried to feel something but nothing would come. He couldn't have been that bad. There's that postcard, the blue water hissing now in the flames and the word 'generic'

16

in the odd place, gone for ever. So really, she'd never actually had an affair.)

And now she was terrified because nothing could ever be the same again, nothing, day nor night nor season, nor logic nor sense. The day was Thursday. She went back to her design job four days later. They had met once again. On Friday his wife had joined him. It hadn't, after all, been his place, he had the key to his friend's flat for when he was working in these parts. Even this became an intimate revelation. Because it was the weekend, and such a beautiful one, his wife was joining him to spend it by the sea. What sea? Beatrice had forgotten the Atlantic behind her. Her husband, R, joined her also and as far as she could remember, they talked normally.

On Saturday at a quarter past five Beatrice managed a quick hour in the pub. From the newsagent's she had spotted Him at the door, pecking his nurse wife goodbye, she who was obviously on the way to the beach. Beatrice told her husband, with unmannerly haste, that she was going to head off alone for a walk. She wouldn't be long. He said OK. Beatrice followed Him into the pub. 'Oh goody,' he said. 'I like furtive women.' They did not strip each other in the pub because you have to be careful about these things. She stayed one hour and left quickly when she saw her by-now-perplexed husband walking past the window.

JUNE THE NEXT YEAR
I packed and met my friend in the Pembroke for lunch. She knows, so she gave me this diary as a joke so I can record the best and

*the worst, as if I would. I have ten days, in the middle of which
R will join me for the weekend. R, my husband, don't, don't hassle
me. The train went through the usual places, which should be
settling, but train journeys always fill me up. Will this throw my
whole life into a sickening chaos? I have to hope that it won't,
I have to hope that it will. That's why it would be better not to
find out. Will we be able to speak to each other, will we be able
to talk to each other? But first of all, will I be able to speak at all
and will I give it away by not being able to do anything but stam-
mer and swallow? Or should I say, will he like me as much as
I like him? I am doing this because . . . I wish the train journey
was over. I have one definite arrangement but the rest may be tor-
ture for me. I may become a sixteen-year-old unwoman waiting
to be wanted. Ah no! He is not cruel. Hopefully. I don't have to
mean 'hopefully'. I don't believe that men you sleep with once then
become cruel. Well, why am I thinking this nonsense then? I spent
the rest of the journey seeing him seeing me.*

*My B&B is quite all right. Passed the day being nervous and
wishing I had half a dozen children to occupy me. I am to meet
him at six o'clock. That will give us time. I wish it was five to
six, it's only four. I went to the pub at three minutes to six and
he wasn't there of course, so I went to the toilet and spoke out
loud to myself as if I was talking to him. If you do that to me I
will die. Honestly I will. I knew that I should have been saying,
if you do that to me I will kill you, but that's not what came out.
Went down again. Sat at bar, with my back to the door, in a
delighted nervous mess. He came in and I couldn't look, my eyes
burned so much. My face took on a life of its own. I smiled, then
I looked, he thought I looked lovely and he meant that it was great
to see me and I knew why I was there. He didn't touch me and*

I thought I would split open for the want of his skin. Then it dawned on me that he thought it was his prerogative to touch me first. We talked through an hour, he has had it with marriage, houses, monogamy. Up to his neck, he says. Up to those beautiful balls of yours, I would have thought, if I hadn't been too polite. I was less worried by marriage than he, less immersed in its point- lessness. As he got gloomier I realised that I thought of mine as the state of having or being an identical twin. I suppose that meant mine wasn't working. We were thinking too like people who were not with each other, so we had brandy. I got down from my stool to pay for it, which was not necessary, and made sure that I touched his leg accidentally as I sat back up. That released us from a dreadful wondering, wondering whether the life we'd just described could possibly be ours and if so how had we let it happen? One touch and we were free. We couldn't wait to finish the brandy. The man beside me didn't want his wife to hang up her coat, fur, on the back of the door. Anyone could lift it, he said. She was needled, she was out for a drink, she reminded him, and couldn't give a fuck about the coat.

They went to 'his' place – it wasn't, he had the key and stayed there when he was working around here. His friend who owned it was away a lot, mostly in Belfast doing a course in peace studies in . . .

'Yes, you told me,' she said intimately.

He looked surprised, wary almost. He couldn't remember telling her.

'Last year.'

'Oh yes.'

She didn't have an orgasm, which was very unlike her,

she could usually have one just thinking. A blessing perhaps, or maybe not. She tried to get him to help her, which was new to her. He was reluctant. He got up from the bed quickly and said, 'You women are always so superior, holding back.'

She could have said one of many things. Touchy, aren't we? might have sufficed as the kindest one of them. What she said was, 'Just you wait until the next time.' That relaxed him. He wanted to go back to the pub, so they went.

Morning came as if it and they had been together for ever. But he left, mid-sentence, to work, leaving the oddest non-arrangement hanging between them. She could ring him up at half four at work and then he'd see how he was fixed.

I went to the newsagent's, bought a book and waited in the B&B. And waited some more. I read, pausing now and then as the tips of my nipples sent a glandular earthquake rolling down inside me. So inside me. I have just eaten and it is now four o'clock. I can ring him soon. Can, am allowed to. Dear me, what a long way down. I tell myself that I am not nervous, that instead I have a quiet glow. Not an ecstatic one, a quiet one. This glow makes my life easier, seem easier, I'm thinking about my real life at the moment and, because this glow is part of it, it's not so bad. But I'm not confident that he will want to see me tonight. The lack of confidence on my part is not without cause, he doesn't exactly throw the compliments around. He prefers, 'Just like all the women I know', to 'Do you?' or 'Yes?' or 'Really?'. But then he looked so sorry when I said that R was going to join me, genuinely sorry, I blushed it was so obvious. And he rang his friend to let him know that 'we' were there, not just him. He didn't have to do that, it was definitely showing off. Would it be better if it were after half four? But uncertainty has its own enjoyment, I can feel a wetness inside me and I suddenly have to tighten myself into a shiver.

'I'll be finished here at half five. You could meet me and we could drive up to this other job that I have to check before we decide what to do.' We. 'Fine,' I say, knowing in my heart that I'm too old, good, bright, or something, to be so grateful.

I see the church clock on my way, oh no, oh no, my watch is slow. Will I ever see him again? Ever? Surely he won't have waited, surely he won't, but he had. I would never have had the nerve to be late, I never do, but maybe it was no harm to have kept him waiting, as long as it has turned out all right. Drove to his job, I waited outside, for a minute I imagined that I had been married to him for years. He came out and said, do you want one of the best pints of Guinness in Ireland? Yes, I said. But I wish to God I knew whether we will go to bed or not. He has the control, this is how he likes it, he's not the sort to like it otherwise. I will have to wait. First, call at his (friend's) flat, he jumps out of the car, 'Right. Immersion on, water flowers, will be with you in a minute.' Water flowers! That's telling me something, I wish I knew what. 'Now for the Guinness.' He smiles at me, innocently. I'm confused.

Somewhere after too much drink he hints that we might. I'm nearly sober enough to realise that it is a hint and to wish he had said it earlier but nearly drunk enough to get mad. My passion has been stopped from too much careless yoyoing. We go back, he has a bath, we do. He raises my legs too high, I cannot feel him properly inside like that, I cannot find a touching place for my head. I cannot think this way, I do not care. Am I afraid? I cannot talk to him, he would sniff at my words, talk would be too personal for him, he is on top. Then he gave me a scarf that he used to

21

wear to the dole when life was not so good. 'Here,' he said, 'have this.' Yes, rolled off the bed, off me, let's be precise, and handed me a silk scarf that was sitting on the top of his overnight bag. 'Wear it, it will look lovely on you.' He has left me somewhere I'm not used to being. I say something which makes him laugh a lot, I cannot remember what it was, even as he laughs I have forgotten. However, I am glad that I can make him laugh. Eventually I leave and go back to my booked accommodation, he did not ask me to stay, he wants to see me tomorrow. I am glad to get into a bed on my own. Will I try it again? Of course I will.

Beatrice and he spent three evenings together, each one organised at the last minute. That shouldn't have mattered but it did, it piled up undignity.

On the fourth day, R arrived. He and Beatrice went for a drive, after he had consulted the map. They had a drink and she insisted on talking about this man she had met yesterday, she couldn't help it. He says he can't possibly support the Provos any more. That he used to, although he never believed in war. Now he simply can't. R says sarcastically, looks like they've lost a valuable ally, a supporter who didn't believe in war. Must have suffered from a lot of agonised dissonance. She says, forget it. He says, no, come on, tell me why the man can't, any more. Enniskillen, she says. But that happened ages ago, did the man hear about it late? R is alert and watchful. She had better be careful. She gets even drunker and talks about people reaching the edge and about the ferocious pleasure that unacceptable behaviour can bring to a person. She talks too much and gives out bits of information but R doesn't notice or pretends not to. Maybe he's saving it up. Next morning R and Beatrice make an unembarrassed coupling, easy as a kiss. It's what they do sometimes, help themselves to each other and let the other do the same. R went back to Dublin at the appointed time, leaving an open sea behind him.

Spent the day checking myself. Why am I doing this? To hear myself described, that's it. In both words and involuntary sounds. I enjoy the agony? Maybe I should take up building houses or something else strenuous, maybe heavy gardening? I remember how the kiss shot needles, I remember the exact sound of his moan when I kissed him first. I want to find new explanations, I don't need words for emotions that I don't know, but for the rest, yes. I want to hear him say confidentially to the barman as he asks, too late, for a carryout, 'Ah we only see each other twice a year', and to another, 'My wife likes lots of ice'. I want to be in this. I do not see him as in a film. Many times I walk as in a film, watching me, wondering what will happen next, if anything, but when I'm with him it's not watchable, it is. We have no past, will have no future, we will be bigger, brighter than any regrettable thing. But yet it's only my part in it because I have no intention of telling him, he would only think that I was trying to get us involved. I have no perception of him hearing me. My dear.

Beatrice also spent some moments trying not to think of his wife and her own husband. It was easier not to think of her own husband. In the end she took the easy way out and flippantly thought that if they weren't doing the same thing, it wasn't her fault. That would do for now, now being the time before consequences.

I rang him to arrange where we would meet. He mentioned DB's, where we had met before. He said, 'You know where that is?' 'As if I could forget,' I said with silver in my voice. 'Silly girl,' he said in a downturned tone. Again, I had left myself open for that. I felt like saying, who the fuck do you think you are? but I didn't. (Later when I told him what I had wanted to say he smiled deliciously. 'I expected that,' he said. Ah! so he is wanting someone open and vulnerable, who will wince, against whom he will appear ever, ever so strong. I was also silly enough to ask if he had ever brought anyone else to this flat. He said, in a high voice, 'I've had the key for eighteen months.' That was just a fleeting something in me, a wish for one little thing from him.)

I turned up at DB's with all my stuff. I had decided to presume, now that R had been and gone, that I would stay for the rest of the time with him or else I had decided to be reckless, I don't know. He twitched when he saw my bag. A man sat with us, a friend of his whom he'd just bumped into, he was waiting for a woman to turn up and it was quite obvious that she wasn't going to. He was downcast. My man didn't look too upbeat about his woman, who had. The night was spent, used up, talking to this stood-up man.

We left the pub, he said crossly, 'I'll carry that', taking my bag from me. If I'd insisted that I do it myself, my voice might have wavered, such was the humiliation, embarrassment. I wanted to say, look, I am . . . whatever and I don't usually turn up to stay uninvited but I thought that in the circumstances . . . But when we got outside the pub he crooked his arm and beckoned me to link him. I put my arm in and found myself holding tight. 'Now,' he said, satisfied. I was afraid of such fickleness. He turned the key; I dropped my link because it felt too familiar, let my hand fall into the cold, he turned from the open door and picked it up as if it was his.

He fussed around the settee, the table, making me comfortable, sensing my unease . . . And then he said, 'First I must ring my wife.' The flat had two large windows, both of them dirty. There was an opening between the bedsitting room and the kitchen, supposedly making separate rooms. I went to the kitchen and tried not to hear but I felt like a keyhole-listener as surely as if I'd had my back bent and my ear pressed. I couldn't see out the window. I raged to myself — talk to your heart's fucking content with some boring stood-up thirty-three-year-old, and as for ringing up your wife, stop trying to impress me. I bet you have the year loaded up with planned weekends, otherwise the two of you would go mad looking at each other. I bet you have ducks flying up your sitting room wall, I bet your bathroom is painted pink or powder blue, I bet you think the alcove at the top of the chipboard built-in cupboard is a feature, in fact that's why the two of you bought the house. I bet you moved out the furry animals from the back window of the car just for me. But worst of all, none of this is my business. Nothing about you is my business.

The extremity of my pathetic gratefulness in the face of his sourness was about to blow up. I simply could not listen any longer, nor could I bear to know that I knew what he would say to me if I tried to explain and that before he had it said I would have forgiven him. In truth, I would have liked to have said goodbye, to put his elbows into my hands and kiss him on the mouth. I wrote a quick 'Sorry I couldn't stay. See you sometime' note. I let myself out quietly and was booked into the nearest B&B before he had got off the phone, I bet. I curled up in bed like an armadillo. All night I heard the sound of seagulls out there being plaintive, scratching the sky as if it was glass. If only it was winter I might be blessed with a quiet body. If the fires were lit in rooms, they might take some of the heat out of me.

Beatrice had to wonder for a while why she had done it. There had been the lush devouring, the agile taste of mouths in the morning, long arched fingers moving slowly in the right places. She knew what it hadn't been, she would not have held him just for the sake of holding him. As well as that, she said in conversation, 'yes indeed' when really she meant 'no'. She had never smiled at him without knowing that she was doing it, she would never have told him the truth. But surely there was no need for him to demolish it so completely. Yet there was, a terrible need.

Beatrice tried to get her imagination to mend the holes in her understanding. She knew he had loved her passion when it opened as is necessary but he had found it unacceptable, too uninnocent. I even guided his hand, she thought. Not only that, she had switched the light back on after he had turned it off. And she had kept her eyes wide open. Wider.

Oh, why not take the blame myself? she thought, days cannot do things of their own accord. It was worth it to remember herself in a straight blue dress, a zip from the top to three-quarters way down, a slit from the bottom to join the zip. Even in the dark she liked new cities.

DAY EVERY DAY
Went away to my town with R. The water in the sea, for that, after all, is all it is, was white with cold.

26

It was the beginning of a long weekend, and long weekends can be lonely, or good, or dangerous. The children were going by sea with their father to visit their paternal grand-parents.

Chrissie got up early to do dreadful things, commit sacri-fices to an image that she had never wanted. But she would prove to them that she could have children with polished shoes and matching clothes. Before she woke them she had early morning sickness not only from too little sleep, too many cigarettes, but as a monument to her motherhood. Having once learned the relief of contracting her stomach muscles, she could do it now at will and so, when anxious, edge her way better into the day ahead. She didn't fit her hand into the shoes, as she blacked, marooned and browned them, because her hand was too big. Blue shirt, navy blue jumper and denim for the oldest, pale yellow shirt, dark green jumper and denim for the red-haired, the difficult one, white shirt, rust jumper and denim for her favourite.

They ate breakfast then, the older two trying, out of remarkable sensitivity, not to be too excited, the younger one bungling his way right through his mother's heart. She brushed their hairs, hairs that had given her varying degrees of heartburn, and let them fall whatever way they wanted. Black eiderdown, red razors and brown feathery curls. She was a great one for love. She wished he would come soon so

27

she could stop her hands from conjuring over them.

He did. She answered the door to tidiness. Of course, she didn't look at him, but from the corner of her eye she could see ten years of her life and she could smell clean living. He chatted this particular morning because he must have forgotten who she was. She took the children to the cleanest car she would ever see and filed them into the back seat. He checked the front lamp. Her body leaned into his property. She settled them all comfortably, all of them, even the older one, quiet, looking at her, delighted that she was also doing this. She was nearly overcome by clean car smell, the soft music from perfect speakers, not a wire out of place, the dust-free comfort, as in the cars of rich people, or young men excited with their purchase. She moved their clothes, moved them, rearranged so she could smell this for longer. She could go away on a date in a car like this. Jesus, Chrissie, where are your morals? Just for comfort.

She pulled her body and life out of his success, waved goodbye and said, 'Well, now you're free Chrissie. Do. Do.' She had not relearned yet that people were allowed minutes or days to make plans. She stepped inside. The house was a space enclosed of function with nothing to function about. A craziness came into her soul and she went to the boat to peep-tom on her own children and their father parking the car and leaving the island.

She did not look like a woman who was hiding and she placed herself in the waiting room for the perfect view of the people and the matters which were her concern. A man and his children passed before her. The man was not talking to the children because he was organising tickets, safety and time. The children tottered behind him, plodding aimlessly on to the boat, not sure of what navigation meant. Those were her children.

Excuse me, sir – those children there. They grew to outrageous sizes in my womb and split me open in order to get out. In time my body healed a little. Now they break my heart but it's my cunt that cries. That man with them was my husband. He was, I suppose still is, English and a class up from me on top of that. We went on our honeymoon to see his parents. Can you imagine that for a honeymoon? Mind you, I was dying to see his parents because of the romance. He hadn't told them he was getting married so I was welcomed first as a nice Irish friend, then I went outside to the apple blossom while he told them the news. It had nothing to do with me. They and he then brought me in and gave me tea, welcoming me, I suppose as a wife (which I hated), his mother shocked but still, she gave me sympathetic looks. The sleeping arrangements were changed with the heavy-footedness that should be reserved only for funerals. It was a cruel thing to do to her but I went along with it because I was dazzled by him and hadn't grown up. How desperate, how terrible, sir, that there is not even a nod of friendship left after all that dazzlement.

One of the passing men looked at her – he could have sworn that she was talking to herself. She wore a black coat and a golden scarf. Her eyes pierced holes in her heart. That time, her parents-in-law – the first time the law had any bearing on her life – took a photo of them, her and their son. She couldn't remember which of the parents had held the camera. She had worn a machine-knit cardigan that reached to her knees and had a four-inch waistband. The sister of a woman at work had knit it along with hundreds

of others and had made a fortune. She then got a brain
tumour and died. These facts were there, immovable from
memory. Facts were such harsh things. They could not be
changed. Not even the frills of them could be turned about
to make it easier. His mother had fussed a little but then
got to like her. Chrissie, rather strange name. His young
sister had said that she had two chins. It was a good honeymoon, she thought, although she had nothing to compare
it with.

They had come back and moved into a house that he had
found. Her heart was nearly crushed by the symmetry of
the street. It took her months to know which house was
hers. She talked about this as if it was, what indeed it was,
the greatest crime committed against her to date. But it was
only a beginning. In no time at all she was a dormitory
sleeper giving out breast milk and sex. The men ran out of
the houses into the morning, into cars, and zoomed away
to life, glad to be out of that mêlée for a while. She wore
a dressing-gown late and tried to sleep her life away with
the babies. Sometimes he said, 'You can have the car, I'm
getting a lift today', or 'You can have the car, I don't need
it today', and she let it sit there in the garage because she
had nowhere to go – she was with babies. On those days
she sometimes fidgeted with the car keys absently.

There he was now, on the way up the gangplank. There
they were, her babies, being led away like lambs to people
they didn't know, because of the law. That red hair was her
brother's.

When she said she was leaving 'this good house' to go
live in a dump, he said, 'Not with my children you're not.'

'Yes I am,' she said. 'And they're my children.'

She had a point. Then he said that none of the children were his. This was a man's privilege – they are, they aren't, they are, they aren't. So she said, 'Yes they are all your children.'

These days he kept telling each of them how like himself they were. Panic, she presumed. They were gone into the stomach of the boat and she could do nothing now but be free.

This holiday, he intended to wipe her out for a week. His parents would not mention her and gradually the children would stop talking of her because they would learn that they got no response. He would bring them to clean places, his father's car would be spotless and Chrissie's favourite would long for the hole in his uncle's car that his mother sometimes borrowed, through which he could see the road. Chrissie's favourite would also think that they didn't even want him to talk about her, but what else was there to talk about? He would become quiet. Chrissie's husband had ideas about how to get rid of Chrissie out of her children's heads – all of these ideas taking as their central point, money, tidiness and other states related to tidiness. Surely if he showed them the proper way to live, they would forget about her with her unabashed poverty, her steeliness in the face of what they would not have had to suffer if she'd behaved herself. But would they forget her dreams? He would try. This holiday he would succeed.

Chrissie heard him thinking hate down the gangplank, through the waiting room, into her bones. Still, she could hardly complain. In her bitterer days she had passed

31

through a town where he'd brought them once. They had previously told her about it with rushed excitement. Now she was going through this town on a train, unexpectedly. The name jumped at her, tearing ribbons in her stomach. She frantically talked to all three of them at the same time, gorging them into her, so that they wouldn't become distracted by him. On the way back, going through the town again, she relented and they smiled at her, one single long smile, for remembering. She had looked out the window far away, far away, letting her eyes fill up again, the name of the town giving her a headache. She walked away from the pier. The woman in the black coat and the golden scarf with her hands in her pockets fidgeting for the need of something between them, a blanket, a pan or a child.

Sir, if only I hadn't had them. Can you imagine how I would look, how I would be? If you can, you've a better imagination than me. And maybe it's not imagination you've got because, after all, I do remember not having them – do remember me. You don't even know me now nor then. Still, they're not really children, they're my children. Indeed you're right, sir, they would have had, could have had, a different life if I had not been foolish. But who are you to say that I am a saleable life to be traded against what you call a normal home? My next-door neighbour's son – eighteen – was a vegetarian. His father, one Sunday, cornered him and tried to force meat down his throat. I heard the screams but thought that they could not possibly be coming from our street. It changed my mind about normality.

Another man could have sworn that the woman said something to him.

No, sir, I'm afraid I didn't speak to you.

32

She swung past him, her face showing a brilliant contempt.

Contempt like this is living art, sir. If only I hadn't had them I could go now, and be gone when he came back and never have to see him again, which is, after all, what the whole thing was about. My babies. My poor dear babies. How could I think them out of existence? Once though, I bumped into my husband on the street. We both nearly stopped, forgetting for a split second the last seven years, not remembering for a tiny flash that we hated each other. We said hello because it was too late not to, then we sprang as if burned, up the street in opposite directions, which is the way we should always have been going. I thought sorrow, vengeance, then pity-for-me who couldn't go, stuck on an island full of catholics because of a husband. Sir.

When Chrissie got home she noticed the dead crocuses. They lay flat in the window boxes like purple, yellow and white snails' slime and they drew her down with them, even though their obviousness should have been dismissible.

Because such darkness does not have survivors to tell tales, Chrissie woke next morning, Sunday, with a new approach floating in her dreams. She went walking in the park wearing a red jacket, a silver scarf, and carelessly twiddled a daffodil. But the park was full of men with children. Men who ten years previously would have been in pubs at this time, drinking their Sunday morning pint before going home to dinner and the wife. Now they were embarrassedly running round after the children, putting them awkwardly on swings, exercising their rights. She had never been that fond of parks, but today this one was particulary bad, even worse than normal – it had become the exchange point. Mostly mischievous children, who knew when big people had had it up to there, and some serious, hardened children were passed from one sullen parent to another. In that brief moment, the parents, big children one and all, tried to hold on to dignity, self-righteousness and contempt – poor excuses for what was once love. The mischievous children took advantage of the moment before being whipped into line by the receiving parent, who didn't wish to appear out of control. Chrissie sidled out of the park as if it had nothing to do with her and she was just a normal Sunday-morning woman thinking about lust.

At the bus stop a child had well and truly got the better of her father – she was eight, he was forty:

'I'm going to tell Mammy.'

'Fucking tell your Mammy whatever you like. You just do that.'

You'd think he was talking to a six-footer.

'Yes. Just do that.' He caught his chest. 'She has me heart broke. Her effin' mother, excuse the language, has her ruined.'

Chrissie's approach for positivity was getting buffeted on the outside so she headed for home again.

Why couldn't she have put up with it – what was so difficult about One House, One Man? She'd done everything else for him, sat on a chair one night thinking just that, feeling an intra-uterine device sear through her insides up to her tonsils. It was only supposed to be for the lower, the dangerous, regions, but it left its pains in every other part of her body too. The doctor had talked about politics as she embedded the foreign object in her pink womb. That helped

Chrissie not to think of the mutilation and the pain. When she had met him first she had gone to bed a lot between letters, taking their love with her and hiding it under the blankets, even wrapping it inside her so no one could steal it from her. How more faithful could she have been? She had rung his telephone number even when she knew he wasn't there just to hear it ring. Hadn't she had children for him? For him. Certainly it could not have been for herself. How much more could she have done? In the first year when they fought she said she was sorry, always sorry, and meant it. Later when they fought, she put her arms tight around the baby and made an outsider of him. It was her only possible defence against the words of a healthy man. They walked home one time, she pleaded for a taxi as her monthly blood seeped from her insides, he, with the money in his pocket, refused. He thought that she would forget that. Chrissie found it hard to remember now the love that must have been there. Every time the word came unbidden she flicked her eyes as if she were a train timeboard. Move on. She had written a message for him once on a dusty bus, that much she did allow herself to think upon: 'If you pass here you'll have walked the same steps as me. Love, Chrissie.'

When he had got the divorce papers she was raging that she hadn't thought of it first or even had had one procured by using a friend's London address, and she could have said, you moron. I did that years ago. He would have got the papers in a serious fashion, in his own country, she could just see him, as if cutting out something distasteful. She would have done it in style and gone for wine afterwards.

35

Her children. Where are they now? Liking the sea, she hoped. Not afraid, she hoped. Last week the middle one had said, 'We have this couch in our father's. You can make a bed out of it.'

'Do you indeed, and is it black leather and does it have a silver spring and is the shape of a pregnant woman's body branded on it?'

'What did you say, Mammy?'

'Nothing.'

'And we have this tape.'

'Really! And is there a song on it called "Make Me an Island"? Ha!'

'How did you know that?'

She slammed the door: my couch! And the next door: my tape! By Jesus, wait until your twenty-first. See that corner, I'm going to get you into it and tell you about your precious father. I wouldn't want to do it for a while, ten or fifteen years or so, because I'd be afraid of deranging you or giving you a complex. What I do to save your mental health and your ego! But it will keep. This corner here. And you'll know then from where I get this tight lip that gets tighter by the month. This corner. That is if we're still in this flat, of course. And if it matters then.

On Sundays before and after the first was born, but not after the second, they used to go visiting. Sunday morning loveliness first, reminiscent in its own way of polished shoes and purity. Sex somewhere between twelve and two. Dinner before or after. Never as good as mother's. Not even once. Then fear would descend upon her. The weekend was over now – Sunday afternoon could not offer any opium,

any panacea. Monday isolation loomed and she wouldn't
see anyone for another week. So she would inveigle him
to go visiting on the pretext that a drive would be good after
their lovemaking. He would have wanted to sleep. First
year, they would head either for C and R's or P and K's
– next year, they headed more often for P and K's because
P had a baby too. Third year, equal again because R had
a child now. C and R were different from P and K in smallish
ways, not in any major way that one expects from our belief
that the individual is unique. (Not to mention the set of two
individuals.) C and R bought a dearer suite of furniture but
P and K spent what they had saved by buying the plastic
suite on a superior three-in-one hi-fi set. Both C and R and
P and K bought dining-room suites, washing machines and
do-it-themselves combinations on/in which to store their
wedding presents. Chrissie would sit dazed. She never
knew the difference between makes of food-mixers and was
deficient in her appreciation of woods. Should they have
stayed at home? Perhaps if they had, C and R or P and K
might have visited them in the way that frightened young
married couples will drop in on each other to check that
things have not gone too far wrong. At least in her own home
she could have had some control over the conversation.

'When is the baby due, Chrissie?'

'What baby?' She felt her womb and pretended she'd
thought it was someone else they were asking about. 'Sorry,
me? oh me, eh, four months.'

Whose house was she in? Was it C and R's or P and K's?
They would then drive home, or rather her husband would
drive home and she would look out the window at Sunday

visitors who had been out looking for people like themselves, some of them successful, some of them unsuccessful, missing-passing the people they were looking for on both journeys, as they — the people they were looking for — looked for them and missed-passed them. She hadn't seen C and R or P and K since. Wonder what they were like now? Would she have even one word to say to them? Probably one hundred and sixteen Sunday afternoons. Each.

Her children would be there by now.

'Daddy's taking us to Ingaland. Why do you never take us there, Mammy?'

There were three possible answers to that and then the real one. She opted for silence.

Once they had gone to a hotel to meet some manager or other from her husband's job. She sat on the soft seat looking at the glass doors, at cars, and porters, at excitement, at sex, at beauty. Her husband ranted and railed about privilege, about class. Who was he to talk? She knew nothing about these things, only about freedom. The manger or other joined them, she still looked out the glass doors. Lights, car lights, were coming on, cheating the summer night. The excitement was getting hotter.

'What did you say, Chrissie?'

'Sorry, nothing. Excuse me I must go to . . .' Jesus, the toilets were fit for living in.

Freshen your mouth right now. Twenty p for a pre-pasted toothbrush.

Imagine! She hoped she had two tens. She did. How could she remember it, that brush? It was blue plastic with a screw-on top, a plastic brush, a smell of fresh toothpaste.

It was travel, travel bags, trains, talking to strangers, new cities, flat hot countries, mirages. She put it in her bag for when she would need it. It was that, and that sort of thing, which made her leave 'this good house', 'the good house', 'your home'. She forgot for a moment in the saying of it that she had three children and by then it was too late. Still, they were the only mistake she hadn't made. Her time would come.

'You're forcing me to consider hitting you.' That was worse, only in some senses, than being hit. She waited to be hit. She never was, just starved. But her time would come some day for revenge.

By the day of the actual split she was so tired that all she ever thought of was sleep. The split itself wasn't such a big thing to her at all. As things had deteriorated to a noticeable level, relatives started calling on her, during the day, anything to stop the whole thing from falling apart. Anything. At least she wasn't on her own any more. Maybe if they'd done it sooner? She wished she had the nerve to ask them to let her go to bed for a short sleep, just a little sleep, instead of talking to her. Now that they were here, could they mind the children for an hour? Immediately they'd come in the door, she'd think of her bed. Remember that Sunday they'd joined the queue for parking cars outside the church, like any other suburban couple with the country mother in the front seat beside the man, the driver, the daughter or daughter-in-law in the back? When the rumpus erupted because they'd missed mass – the times had been changed six months before – Chrissie was fast asleep. The sun streamed in on her and, despite the annoyance, they let her sleep on, her mother nearly sympathetic.

She decided to clean the house – always better than remembering, and it came naturally to her now, but she knew that it was daft to do housework when she wasn't confined. Yet what could she do? In the end she used the long weekend to feel sorry for herself sometimes, with good reason (it was also therapeutic and it saved her from feeling inadequate), and the rest of the time to become a new Chrissie yet again. She talked to herself, went for walks dressed in white, black, purple, told secrets to the one tree in the avenue, and kicked expensive cars on her way home at night. By the time they came back, half of her wanted to squeeze radiance into their faces, another half would have passed them in the street and pretended it had run away from home. But her favourite smiled first and that settled that.

A LITTLE REMOTE

She left her job and her organised life with an ease that surprised herself more than anyone else. It was martyrdom, but it didn't feel like it. Lucy Skipplestow was off to mind her widowed, retired businessman father. The sea would be there. The west coast of Ireland greyness might lodge in her brain, in the winter damp it might burrow into her bones, but when the sun shone she could think herself anywhere. Sometimes the sky and the sea were one, there. The ocean was the clouds and the grey clouds were really seaweed. A skyful of white foam stretching for all the visible miles can make anyone's day seem more important than it is. Lucy should not have gone back so easily – she should have been more concerned about her job, her flat, her life – but something other than guilt made her.

Friends would take over her rooms, it would always be there for her, her reference was eulogistic. Her life could wait. What much was it anyway? A lover here and there, often more trouble than they were worth. She could have fun and friends anywhere, because what was the difference between one shared laugh and another, one chat and another? So she told herself. She didn't dwell on her belief that it probably wouldn't be for long. She had set his death scene long before the thought had entered his head or his body. Lucy, blessed with unusual luck, had said what she had to say to her mother before she died. She needed to say something to Mr Skipplestow or at least to try.

She did try, but he wasn't used to listening to other people, certainly not women. His life had always been a business, time was a profit or a loss. He would have built a bunker for investment in it, but people might have laughed at him. Anyway, he would surely be able to die a natural death, and Lucy should look after herself. So she cooked for him and drove him, washed and prepared his food, living in separate blocks which came together to make a day, a week, a month, in the receding life of Mr Skipplestow. (And Lucy.)

She returned happily to an old hobby and discovered that she was better at it than she had remembered. She painted large pictures in her room on canvases that were sometimes a foot taller than herself. She stretched to put in stars and birds or peered at yellow whins and wondered if they were maybe too golden. She smiled a lot to herself each time she finished a picture.

In the beginning she bought frames only when she was shopping alone. Then she chose them with her father. Later, Mr Skipplestow bought them for her, not for any serious reason, but because there was not much point in painting pictures if you didn't frame them. Once, he looked at some of the canvases in her room. He was surprised that there were so many of them. Lucy liked the smell of paint and it passed some time. She would not get notions about herself.

When her father's brother died, she prepared to go to the funeral with a little excitement. A night in her old flat in Dublin, the boat journey to Holyhead, a train speeding to

London. She arranged to meet Bernard on her way back. She would be gone for almost a week and the funeral didn't really bother her because she had not been close to her uncle.

Her flat startled her in some way. She stood in the doorway and thought about the strange ways she'd grown up inside these rooms. She had experienced ecstasy, small pieces of love, and some loneliness here. Past experiences became animate objects and seemed to look down on her from the corners of the ceilings. Her friends were keeping it well. They all went for a drink. There were people everywhere, Lucy got drunk on them. There were friends of hers from minor pasts that she'd forgotten about – it's funny how many pasts a person can have and it still makes only one. They were all here to see her, up from the country, which made her worry that perhaps she was doing an odd thing. Was it really so? She worried that perhaps it was. There were so many people, so many people, to pick from. She could talk to any of them, any one of them, and there would be more after that. How wonderful! Was there a time in her life when she had kissed strange men? Been kissed and more? When she had herself taken initiatives, despite the risks of being turned down? Had she once bought satin sheets? Surely not! She felt awkward among these people who were at ease carnally with each other – you could tell, they moved their bodies past and around themselves without saying excuse me. Back in the spare room she fell asleep quickly, protecting herself from too much wondering.

It was a relief to get on the boat, to be pulled away from the shore. What was the difference between her now and one year ago? Could it be that strange? Could she have become strange? She would have time to think. She supposed there was not much point in thinking about the painting.

The boat smelled of recent vomiting, but the sea was kind on this journey. Lucy bought a ticket for the Pullman lounge and sat with the individuals on the boat, the people who had big jobs, big cars, and big everythings, away from the emigrants and their conversations. She'd had those on every other journey over. Emigrants always talked, blabbered in fact, terrified that they were making a mistake. Women who didn't talk and looked ahead of themselves were not emigrants. There were always a few of them on the boat, holding themselves together. Lucy read some, slept some, tasting her hangover. She had tea, read some more. She didn't now want to think.

Two men talked loudly; bulging with confidence, she thought bitterly. Should she be minding a man like them beside the sea? Had they or he ever done anything for her? How did they see her, they or he? He saw her, in fact, for her daughterly use. He didn't know much about her, but that didn't bother him. They, these two, didn't notice her at all. They were gone past noticing every woman. Lately they only looked at the ones that they felt they could get without much bother, between matters of a serious nature, on the rare occasions that they were moved to it now.

Lucy was glad to get on the train. Her journey was becoming layered relief. She watched England pass her window, trying not to think about the desolation of Crewe or Chester. But maybe the train stations were giving the wrong impression. Maybe Crewe was full of people in love. Perhaps away from the station there were narrow streets and cosy front rooms. She swallowed the foul-tasting artificial tea – you couldn't cheat by taking tea bags because the cups were pre-filled. She should have thought of a flask. But was she that old? She looked well, all of her, her face in particular. Perhaps her body gestures were a little hurried, she needed to hold back sometimes from something, maybe from disgracing herself.

At Rugby a family boarded. The small girl sat in the now vacant seat beside her. People had come and gone at stations and Lucy had avoided all conversation, but a child was harmless.

'Can I see your book?' She flicked through the child's book. It was a horrifying tale of missionaries and of God's wrath on a black pagan boy. The family were heavy Christian. The child did not trust her, could sense Lucy's doubt about the story. She slunk to the other seat to her father's knee. An older child hissed at her not to disturb him because he was praying. She came back to Lucy's seat.

Could Lucy say anything that might endear her to the girl? She could feel her anger rising at those people, at those parents, who could tell the child whatever they liked, especially in the name of God, because they were parents, funny thing parents, and she Lucy was no one. Her no-oneness silenced her. Why should she care anyway? Who were these people to her? And children?

Later the mother read the story aloud – the black pagan was helped by Christians because he was gradually losing his sight; he did go blind, despite the help, but 'Wasn't he better, dear, to be blind and to know Jesus than to be a pagan?' Whatever you say, you lovely logical adult you. The child looked terrified but she might give up her job when she was older to take care of them; then again she might murder them.

Euston drew towards them rhythmically, as if the train and London were two people rushing towards each other. Passengers jumped out of carriages as if scalded and dashed out exit gates, never once bumping into each other. Lucy was not a bewildered stranger to this station scene. She had been to London often and in fact she loved it. She was also glad to be off the train. Surely that would be the last of the reliefs. Three chirpy people held a banner above their heads. Lucy passed them, then turned curiously to see what she could already hear, an enthusiastic welcome, the sort that always jolts the lone traveller. It was for the Christians. She was disappointed. She met her own relations, shook hands and left for the funeral parlour.

'How is your father?'

Why couldn't they call him by his name?

'Fine.'

'You must find it a little remote?'

'No. Not really. I paint.'

What a thing to say!

The attendant was Irish – not from Dublin. He walked towards the body, his hands down in his pockets, with the awkwardness of a country man in his Sunday suit on a Tuesday. His face was not heart-failure blue, but rather a raw red that had worked its way deeper than skin in a place miles, oh centuries, from here. His reverence and discretion grated on Lucy, yet she knew she should allow him these, as well as his moment of victory, one London Irish standing over one dead London Irish.

Her uncle lay mocking her by the resemblance to her own father. She could hear his voice clearly, now that she saw him before her, a soft London overtone, urging her mother not to be such a square, at some past family gathering. He was the wild one. He had a dimple and it had suited him.

They left the freezing room and made their way to the distant cousins' flat where Lucy would stay. Relations were gathering and were being accommodated here and there with clinical precision. Now that the viewing of the body was over she could look at the colour of London. It was always good for her.

Her distant cousin was having some people to dinner. It had been too late to cancel, so the mourners were mixed with the guests. A lazy stiltedness hampered the free-flow of conversation, but Lucy didn't mind – she was enjoying herself because she could afford to judge lives now that she was away from her own. The man was at the bottom corner of the table, she thought now, but she couldn't be sure because, true, she had not noticed him immediately. Later she drifted into conversation with him. She'd had better conversations in her life; she'd had worse. Some relation whom Lucy had never met interrupted.

'Your father couldn't come. Of course. It's nice for him to have you.' A sad, piqued little voice making some point known only to itself.

The man – Desmond, Desmond Palmer – moved away.

'How do you like the change to the country?' the relation

continued. This person knew everything. Who was he?

'I'm your father's cousin once removed. You remember Francis and Kevin, on holidays? My sons. You were small, of course. Solicitors and doctors now.'

'Oh yes, I do, now that I think about it.'

No word of his other son Brendan. What had he done wrong?

The man Desmond – Desmond Palmer – came back.

'Will it be possible for you to socialise during your stay?'

'I thought that's what I was doing.'

They laughed. The once removed cousin left.

'No, I mean, really socialise.'

'Perhaps the night after tomorrow night. I wasn't close to my uncle.' She had almost forgotten why she was here.

'The night after? Why not come to my house for dinner tomorrow night? The night after seems too late if you only have a few days.'

'Why not.'

Dear Desmond. I wish I could write to you about how I'm feeling, how I'm remembering, but I cannot do that, now that I know you do not feel the same way. You said that women get more hurt out of these things, or was it me who said that? If I was writing to you, I could tell you many things. I could remind you of what you said to me when I said that I wasn't in the habit of doing this. Then again, I probably wouldn't – no, I would leave that aside, why shouldn't I? because no shyness, no fear stopped me, I have no need to make excuses. We didn't know that we didn't know each other. You might think that I have a remarkable memory; I would reply that memory is the vicious tragedy of not being able to forget.

Lucy enjoyed dinner, there was a smell of wine from the sauce. There was music; he had brandy. He had done this before. But no. Well perhaps, well perhaps a few times. They laughed. He told her about bringing his mother back to Ireland. She had not been there since she was twenty. Lucy could see it. He had driven her to the townland. She directed him. She had said that maybe they should stop here and see if this neighbour was still alive. They had asked tactfully. The seventy-five-year-old woman called to the field: 'John, there is someone to see you.' No jealousy left now where there was at least life. John moved away from the scythe, then thought better of it and took it with him so as not to appear too enthusiastic. He and Desmond's mother were eighty-one. He left his hand where it was, cupping grass on the ditch. He squinted at her and drawled in the voice of a twenty-year-old: 'Is that you, Babs?' Then he kissed her, his wrinkled lips touched her cheeks that were well beyond wrinkling any more: 'I've waited sixty years to do that.' They chuckled. She said later 'And he kissed me with his wife standing at the door. Ach well, I suppose.' Outside the cowshed that had been their school. They left after tea and snaps reverently taken.

'I can get you the photo.'

'Do please.'

'This is the house where she was born. Do you know Mayo?' There was a lake in front of the house. His mother had slapped her bag twice on her thigh and said, happy memories, happy memories.

Lucy told him that she painted and that her father read the deaths in the paper every morning. Desmond asked questions about her painting. What colours did she like best? Did she paint mostly people or landscape? Did her women look out? Had she read John Berger? She answered expansively all his questions, all of them, how wonderful to be asked, and yes, she had read John Berger.

They laughed more. They slipped into bed. She touched him but he could only think of being up and inside her. He knew nothing about lovemaking as such, about nearness. Strange, was that why he had shown her the other photographs of his last holiday in Athens? Him surrounded by women. Who was he trying to tell what? I may not be able to make love but I always have a woman. Photographs of holidays at their age! There wasn't much caressing, and what of it there was seemed to be without physical connection, perfunctory rubbing until he could get inside. His own body was cold as steel with only one feeling part to it. The man who had taken his mother back! She tried running her fingers over his shoulders, butterfly movements on his chest. OK then, too light, stronger, stronger touching from his toes to his ears, kiss-sucking his nipples. She shivered. It was like communion with a corpse. All right then, if that's what you want, do please enter. I will take you in and wrap myself around you so you can be safe. And when he did come in he was grateful. He wanted to put out the light.

'Why?' she asked.

'Because if I make love with you without the light on, the dark will never be as bad again.'

'What is your house in the west like?' Desmond asked her in the morning, waking her gently.

'Big windows. Quiet.'

'Your town?'

She could see the Sunday session in the local pub. She didn't want to. Not this morning. Begrudging people. How could she explain, without letting them down, that they were afraid in the summer, when their cruel wintry life came face to face with holiday-makers? It would be a pity to sell them short in this plush room. She said nothing about them and talked instead of blue skies, when they were blue, green fields, the sun, the colour of clothes. Her voice seemed nervous as it came out into the quiet . . .

'I want to be inside you again.'

Dear me, Lucy thought. She felt herself getting into trouble. It seemed as if cloudy bits inside her head were melting, her blood was wet, slipping into places that had been dry for a while; like a teenager, she winced. But where caution warned her she didn't listen.

She did wish him to say more, now that it was daylight, but he had brought her down to his size and didn't need to. (That was caution speaking to her.) Was he going to ask her to stay longer? She might have been expected to feel uncomfortable about some things – for instance, naked bodies, his and hers, the bathroom off the bedroom, french letters, the phone ringing – but the only thing that worried her was, did he want her to stay? Was she lively enough? She went to bed with him again, back to the wombing, because she felt so pleased when he did ask her that it would have been a nonsense not to have. But she felt his silence taking something from her. He could have looked at her all day, all the time, as he moved, hoping to chase away the reluctance in her, but she would not look back. She would not. She turned her head. He was undecided as to whether or not he should feel slighted or encouraged. He opted for the latter and felt worse for it. She withdrew, like a snail, taking her juices with her. Emptiness came into her.

He stopped the car three minutes before they got to her distant cousins' place to show that he was emotional.

'How does that prove anything?' she wondered aloud, perplexed.

'I didn't want to wait until we got there to say goodbye.'

There was a funeral to be gone to.

Desmond Palmer promised to ring Lucy Skipplestow before she left to go home to Ireland. He did not phone. Who knows why not? Lack of interest? Unlikely – some of his words suggested a lot of interest. Fear? Perhaps he thought that emotion was something to be allowed in the over-eighties, if they could still think by then and if they lived that long. Lucy Skipplestow was upset, in fact she was devastated, which she shouldn't have been because she should have known better, but since when has 'shouldn't' been 'isn't' or 'wasn't'?

Dear Desmond. Perhaps you did ring and I was out.

Lucy got on the train in a silent Euston. She hated him. There were curses and rages in her head. She fell asleep exhausted and woke holding his hand. She jumped from the seat to have tea and to shake him off but it was too late now to do that. She thought about nothing else through England, his face came with her the whole way. On the boat she sat on the same lounge seat, away from returning emigrants and still, silent women, yet she could not remember getting off the train.

But Lucy, you thought yourself that the sex was questionable and you have said before that . . .

He was lovely, she thought, bloody lovely.

That woman there, who is painting herself now, an hour from shore, she has had three children, all of them sons. She is painting herself to meet her in-laws. She is happy. Lucy would have to think about having a child, some day.

The steward turned away two children who wanted only to watch television. This was a paying room. He included Lucy in his scathing look to them – he thought she also wanted them gone, but she hadn't even seen them.

Somehow Ireland came into view. A call from ship to shore. Lucy does not wish to be landed.

Her flat seemed more welcoming this time. Lucy was subdued, defeated by chance. She wished she had some cold lever, some device to move her out of this wretchedness. A few days would surely help. She met Bernard – who was he? She focused and refocused her eyes, but could not remember him. He thought her distant and off-putting.

She did not wish to go west. A city at least offered some diversion. But she went, because she would not have to explain her foolishness there.

For a month she watched the postman. She felt a

numbness and at the same time a silliness that was very alive. One morning she nearly prayed.

Dear Desmond. I wish I could phone you but I am afraid. I keep waiting for you to write. I cannot believe that you are not thinking of me at exactly the moments that I am thinking of you, which is, I'm afraid, often. How could you not be?

Seasons ran easily and predictably into each other. Lucy tagged her own life on to her father's. He wasn't, after all, so bad. Really, it wasn't that he didn't want to understand, perhaps he just couldn't. She painted large wild pictures with the women looking out. She often said the man's name when she was stroking on the last blue or yellow.
Desmond.

Dear Desmond. I sometimes think of you naked and how pleased you were. But it gets harder to remember. What is your face like? What colour are your eyes? Strange that you should have tried to impress on me so much that your life was all right, strange that you should have told me that you went to work whistling, an archaeologist, happy with the tenth century and ruins. Strange, because I believe that you are even unhappier than I. Do you have a beard, glasses, hair? I cannot remember.

The evening that she did ring, a year ago now, he sounded half-pleased, flattered, but closed, definitely closed. Lucy knew. Her own voice rang in her ears for hours afterwards,

words like Lucy fool, then she calmed herself, better to
know. He wasn't very brave. He would never have fitted
in around here anyway.

Summer was good. The dry clouds lit up at night in pink
and orange stripes. The traditional musicians played with
less cocksuredness, shocked by the sun and the way it gave
the women some extra secret. They changed to slow tunes
because reels were made for winter. Lucy put some of the
musicians under a pink cloud in a painting. She stood at
the big quiet window wondering about colour, her legs a
little apart. Normally she didn't notice how she stood but
this morning she felt him between her thighs, the whole
body of him, so she knew her feet must be apart. She felt
him distinctly and heard his need to be inside. Her lips
thinned, moved to the ends of her mouth, her eyes crinkled
at the corners. It could have been called a smile. And then
the pain came back, the memory of his eyes, that was the
worst because it was so personal. Looking is very personal,
Lucy thought.

Dear Desmond. Whatever you gave me, you didn't. I gave
it to myself. You're only a tired spawn floating heavily
in me.

Dear Desmond. That's from an old Italian poem. I didn't
mean a word of it.

Her father died in January. He just couldn't pitch himself
at another year. She held his hand and the next minute he
was gone. Her heart split open and every woman and every

man she'd ever loved passed through the crack, hitting off the edges as they went.

By the end of February Lucy had packed all her belongings ready to go back to Dublin. She wondered what the paintings would look like in a confined space, crushed into a city. She had gone to Dublin three times since the death. Bernard had helped her get the flat ready. She wanted to share the rooms with someone because she hoped to get a part-time job until such time as her clock could understand commerce again. Bernard seemed ideal, Lucy told him. He tried to show only the appropriate amount of delight. But first she would have a weekend in London.

Desmond had heard about her father's death, through the distant cousin, and had written her a letter. He was good at things like that, archaeology and old love. She would go now, because since her father's death she felt her full height, five feet eight inches. She decided not to tell Bernard and to leave wondering why not until later. She would be able for whatever did or didn't happen in London. For long enough now Lucy had watched the sun slipping out of the sky into the ocean and she had learned not to cling to it the way a child holds on to the hem of a skirt. In the west she had also learned about colour, old men and exiles.

Dear Desmond. Thank you for your letter. Certainly I'd be delighted to call on you next time I'm in London. As it so happens . . .

Exiles, men on the run, make love to their countrywomen

high up in the womb, which is hard to get over, but Lucy had seen how the sun always comes up again from the other side of the sky and how it spends a whole day shining on skirts.

THE PARK

Apparently my blood pressure is the same as everyone else's, that is, just below boiling point. The fat which, during the last few years, had wrapped itself like a tight hug around my arse, has begun to disappear. Where does fat go when it falls off people? Are there chunks of it floating around the air in the exact spot where people have got thin, and where is the exact spot, and do people breathe it in and does it damage their lungs? My nerves are no worse than they ever were, and I sleep well. These things surprise me but they don't surprise Brigid. Nothing surprises her, that's why I love her, and her eyes are grey.

Brigid was going through a bad time, doing her best to get through each day without making an ass of herself. Her boyfriend (she would call him a lover, because she has confidence like that) was away. Again. But this time there was an eeriness about his absence, an insistence, that seemed to be trying to tell her something. She was finding it difficult to put her days in, days based on promises, particularly since, as she had begun to admit to herself, the promises had never actually been put into words and said. She had a notch up from a middling job in the corporation and the sort of car that a woman like her can afford in a country which, eleven years later, was to miss the point completely and interview the staple diet of men on the night that Mary

Robinson was elected president. She was driving home in this car wondering, and trying not to, if there would be a letter from him when she got there. More of those flags had appeared. This area had been coming down with flags for the past week. New ones sprouted every evening as if there had been multiple births all day long when people who had work were at it. A local festival she presumed, a very spready local festival by the looks of it.

There was a long letter from him that said nothing but wished she was there, which was something. She bit the inside of her lip, wondering again, until it bled. She walked around her flat in a disarrayed fashion, picking things up and putting them down somewhere else. Sheena rang her and asked her if they wanted to go out to dinner tonight.

'It's for Macartan McElwaine, he's emigrating next week, lucky divil.'

'There's no we, only me,' she said.

'Ah, is Diarmuid away again? Well, come yourself.'

Because something is better than nothing, she went. She took the poor-route bus into town, the quickest journey, the one that makes no effort to avoid the desolate patches. She tried not to hear the tightly packed sounds of poverty. Not tonight.

'Your perm's still in.'

'It'd need to be. I only got it done a month next Thursday.'

The restaurant was perfect. It could dismiss the outside world in a matter of seconds. It had the right consistency – ordinary enough to be relaxing, slightly exotic, so Brigid could be interested, a little conservative, so she could count herself exotic in contrast. This hanging between realities made her dizzy with satisfaction.

The others came together. There was Jacinta, a long-term student, who always had money from somewhere and who was more used to spending it in pubs than in restaurants; Sheena, an indifferent clerk in the Norwich Union Insurance Corporation, a dedicated northerner whose mind was sharp as razors; Macartan, dreamy and absent always, but even more so tonight because he was already drinking fast drinks in Manhattan; and Padhraig Copeland, whose father, a Connemara *gaelgeoir*, had married a Basque woman, who sometimes spoke Spanish with an overlay of longing.

They fussed and hugged and sat down and ordered wine and made plenty of noise. They were of the runaway generation. Brigid too. There were no family heirlooms, even cheap ones, in their sitting rooms, because none of them had been forgiven, not yet anyway. Perhaps later they would be, when the death of a parent might force reconciliations on the one left behind. As teenagers they had bitten and sniggered at everything, and when they got to be twenty they didn't have to swallow their words because things were better then.

Brigid liked staring at people. She was mesmerised by their hair, their faces, their clothes. She could see sloppy sewing through an overcoat. Looking at these people, what could she see? Jacinta never had to seek first attention because she had carrot-magenta hair. Since the sixties, when it was first allowed that red could be matched with pink, or other reds, or any colour, Jacinta had started wearing shocking blood lipstick. She wore it still, even though the time had not yet come around again when thinking women could paint themselves. Padhraig Copeland was far too good-looking – there should be a law against anyone having such a perfect face and mouth. No one ever noticed what he was wearing. Macartan McElwaine had a startled face, a crooked nose, and hair so straight it looked wet. Sheena was so puny she nearly had no face at all; therefore her voice came always as a surprise, a big deep thing that had its way perfectly curved around difficult ideas. She had fed her intelligence well. Brigid would have a good night after all.

Sheena was concerned about the impending visit of the pope to Ireland. 'It will knock us back years,' she said.

So that's what all the flags were for. Brigid wondered to herself where the people had got them. Had they had them all the time in boxes, away with the Christmas decorations, waiting in case the pope ever did come to Ireland? Or was there a factory somewhere spewing them out of machines at a rate of knots? Or did the women sew them up at night in their individual homes and pretend that they had had them all along?

'Look how much damage he particularly of all the popes has done, in how many years? How long has he been pope now?'

Jacinta remembered. Exactly. Because she was picked out of a crowd on the night of a Reclaim the Night march in Dublin by a TV personality and asked if she would come on his programme and say how she could defend not letting men go on the march in support of the women's demand that they should be able to walk safely down the streets at any time, day or night, without men. Well, that's not the way the TV personality put it. She said yes. When she got there her knees were knocking together with fright and she had forgotten that television was in colour so her clothes were all wrong (how could she have thought that, her and her shocking blood lipstick?). But she was saved because the first Polish pope ever had just been chosen and *Today Tonight* had spent all evening scouring Dublin for a Polish priest. By the time they got one, all the Polish priests were paralytic on vodka. So there he was, his English not the best in the first place, slurring his way through his interview. In comparison to him, Jacinta sounded like a professional.

Sheena was so concerned at the assumption that we all wanted the pope here she said that something should be done about it. '*We* should do something,' she said.

And that led to a long discussion about what they would do, what they couldn't do, what they could do and what they dared to do.

And so by the end of the meal they had decided to paint slogans, so that people would know there was some opposition in the country. They believed that to be important. Nothing too drastic like 'Fuck the Pope', because that could be taken up the wrong way, twice. Nothing too obscure, because people would just knit their eyebrows and not understand. Something simple like 'No priest state here.' They would do it on the road from Maynooth to Dublin.

'Maynooth,' Macartan said dreamily, turning it on his tongue as a child would repeat a word to itself, knowing that it meant something but not knowing what. 'Maynooth, where priests are made.'

Brigid was given the job of driving down and up to

Maynooth once or twice over the next few days to calculate how many special branch cars were cruising the route. 'Branch cars! How will I know them?'

'You'll feel them on the back of your neck,' Sheena said.

During the week, Brigid dreamt that she was a bird flying into people's kitchens, into canteens, on to building sites, switching the bloody radios off as they built up cosy pictures of the wonderful preparations for the wonderful man, the way a radio voice can.

The night came, the night before he was to come. Brigid felt nervous in an alert way, pleased that they were doing at least some little thing. She had plenty of petrol, oil and water in the car. She had cleaned it while she was at it. The tins of paint were in the boot. She was clean herself, spruced up in a pair of jeans that had zips where no zips were needed, a royal blue, light jumper, a white shirt collar peeping up around the neck.

They had decided to leave her flat after midnight. The later they painted the slogans, the more chance they would remain unnoticed until morning, when people would see them on their way to work and be outraged or smile gleefully with relief. It was a long evening. At twelve o'clock or thereabouts Sheena and Macartan arrived. By half past twelve it was obvious that Jacinta and Padhraig had had second thoughts and were not in favour of pursuing a wildcat decision taken in a restaurant when there had been plenty of wine drunk, all because Macartan was emigrating – oh! yes, leaving the place, but brave enough to do one last thing for the oul' sod before he abandoned it altogether, easy for him. And as for Sheena, she'd think better of it when she remembered her job; and as for Brigid, she'd never.

So Macartan, Sheena and Brigid set out and drove through the early autumn night. Sometimes they checked to see if Brigid's calculations of the branch cars were correct – every eight minutes, every five minutes, that's not one, oh, it is, it is, I can feel it – but mostly they behaved as if they were out on a mid-afternoon Sunday drive.

The first one was the hardest. They reached the spot that Brigid had picked out before they had decided who would do it. They shouted at each other and jumped around in their seats as if a flea had bitten them. But they calmed down and decided that Sheena and Macartan would do the first ones in rota while Brigid sat at the wheel and started the car up again when they got to the second last E. If they were getting on well, she could have a go when they got to a quieter spot.

OK, here goes. NO PRIEST STATE HERE in luminous white paint, lucid in the dark, as if it had been there for all time. They had to tear themselves away. They could have stood around for hours chatting, taking the odd, long, admiring look at it, remarking on how well the letters were done, smelling the paint, watching the moon watching it. The second one, a mile from Maynooth, lacked originality, didn't look as pleasing, but maybe that was because of the bad background wall, which didn't show the letters up terribly well. The straight stretch of characterless road took away from it too. Still, it was done. And a third. By now the rhythm was flawless – they had the paint and brush and painters out and in again in one minute.

They were concentrating so hard on the fourth, enjoying themselves so much, making the letters flourish more, that they didn't hear the car coming until it had rounded the corner ahead of them. Quick as a flash, Brigid switched on the engine and moved forward. The driver would think he had only imagined that the car had been stopped. Macartan and Sheena jumped across the hedge, scratching their legs on thorns. Sheena got stung by a nettle. They sat in the ditch listening to their hearts drumming one long beat in their ears. Brigid drove around the corner, switched off the engine, listened, and when no sound came, she reversed back to the spot. While the two were extricating themselves from the ditch and getting into the car, Brigid, bold as brass, finished off the HERE.

'Phew! If that had happened with our first one, we would have scarpered home.'

Because of the fright, they turned left at Lucan and took the Strawberry Beds road. 'Just as good for commuters in the morning and far safer for this business and more beautiful anyway,' they consoled each other with something near love, born from the fear, that was rising up in their voices. They looked at the road, its tall trees crowded together in places, gossiping, its houses perched dangerously on the edge of steep hills, leaning over to hear. Brigid's mother had walked dogs along this road once, when she worked as a doctor's housekeeper. The dogs were well fed. Had Brigid's mother ever wondered at the beauty? Was she asleep at this moment, having a peculiar dream about the time she worked in Dublin for that doctor?

The drive was so pleasant it was hard to remember that

they had stops to make. Did Brigid's car stop at the very places where her mother had taken a rest with the dogs, listened to the river whispering and making music? Who knows. She couldn't quite remember how many they had done on the Beds road, five at least – she had got to do two herself. The one that stretched across the road, that's the one she liked best, it was under a thick black tree and the RE ran into the roadside, staining the grass as it broke up. It was that grass you can whistle on if you cup it properly between your hand and lips.

They drove homewards talking louder now, laughing a lot at nothing, relief beginning to take them over. They drove up Oxmantown Road, down the North Circular, left at Phibsboro, getting further away, getting nearer a door they could close behind them.

For some reason, they couldn't let it go, this night-time artistry, and they stopped to do one last one opposite the gates of Glasnevin Cemetery. Funny, that was the one that stayed the longest. A Garda car passed them as they drove off.

'Shit, we nearly got caught,' Macartan said.

'Nearly pregnant never did anyone any harm,' Sheena said.

When they got to Brigid's flat they were ravenous. Macartan and Sheena checked the car for stray splashes of paint and washed the brushes. Brigid made fried egg, tomato and mushrooms on toast. Macartan stayed the night.

In the morning they switched stations on the radio. One news bulletin mentioned that some vandals had daubed a protest slogan against the pope's visit.

'*A* slogan, only *one*, is that so?' Brigid said sleepily as she fiddled with the tuner. 'The pope this, the pope that, and the pope the other,' she muttered and switched it off.

By the time they got up, the country was in full swing, children bathed and dressed already if they were travelling far to the park, cars washed, minds battened down, bus tickets secured and picnics packed. People who lived in the city were out buying their plastic chairs. Hawkers were converging on the park. The last stones of the park's inconvenient walls were being tipped into the dump – they had to go to make room for all the cars, guards, priests, mothers, bankers, a few radicals who had decided to make a fortune selling periscopes, councillors, fathers, poets, and musicians who had finely tuned themselves to receive the Body and Blood of Jesus Christ. Those who thought otherwise, were, simply, invisible for the day. By nine o'clock in the morning no amount of floodlights could have picked them out. (It took a certain kind of flash violence to make so many disappear. There are bruises left. There are sounds of strangling. But there you go . . . choking sounds, well, that's only to be expected, it couldn't be avoided . . .)

Brigid's doorbell rang. She went to it slowly because she was feeling the effects of erasure, and the small gurgling of anger in the pit of her stomach was not enough antidote. She opened the door to her smiling brother and his careful girlfriend, her cousins and their friends. They had come early so as to get a good view and to buy some of those chairs if there were any left and they would park their cars here if she didn't mind.

'We thought we'd get our tea here as I'm sure there's no

place open,' her brother said, moving into the hallway.

Brigid felt as if they would crush her if she didn't step aside. She backed into the kitchen. The last one closed the door behind him. They were standing now around Diarmuid's packed luggage. She hated them doing that. That was all she had of him – as long as his belongings were packed in boxes here, here in her room, there was hope. If these pope visitors hung around his things for long, he might never come back. Look at that big ignorant mouth leaning his dirty arse on Diarmuid's stereo. Now that she had woken a little, flashes of anger were skittering through her, shaking her up and strengthening her legs.

She said, 'I'm not making tea for anyone on their way to see the pope.'

They all laughed.

'I'm not,' she said.

They laughed again.

'No really,' she said as the laugh petered out.

Her brother said, 'You were always great crack. I was just saying that recently. We miss your crack in Mullingar, we could be doing with it especially on a Monday morning. Right, who wants tea, who wants coffee?'

Brigid went to the door, opened it, and said, 'I'm serious. No one on their way to the park is welcome here. The whole country is at your disposal today, so why are you bothering me? I'll have enough trouble all day keeping that creep out of my mind without having to feed his followers on their way . . . Enough said, I won't insult you, just get your tea and your posters and your rosary beads somewhere else.'

They did leave, well, what else could they do? their hearts

wincing at the only blow struck against a believer that day. How well it had to be them! Brigid couldn't believe they had actually gone. The triumph left no taste of ashes in her mouth. She said 'Whoopee' and went back to bed with Macartan, where she curled her bare body as close to his as possible, merging her chest into his so their hearts might beat together. He wasn't Diarmuid but he was here. A few hours later they heard a cheer go up from the street. Her neighbours were all hanging out upstairs windows, waving yellow and white flags at a speck in the sky that must be your man's helicopter. Brigid lifted the nearest black garment to hand, which happened to be a nightdress, attached it firmly to her window, and got back into bed again, trying to shut out the noises of belligerent piety.

At half past eleven she and Macartan decided to go to Newgrange, the most pagan place they could think of. They drove alone along roads that wove through north County Dublin townlands, roads that skirted the pope's intended route to Drogheda, meeting the odd branch car, the occupants of which pinned eyes on them – what could those two people be doing? where could they possibly be going? mass was on in the park by now, wasn't it? The pope had already told the people in icy sharp tones what they must not do, and nor must you, and you must not, and also . . .

It would take the people years to recover from the things being said in such a way on such a day. As a million and more genuflected, creeking their knees within a quarter of a second of each other, Macartan put his feet up on the dashboard and sighed the way some of us do when making love has satisfied us beyond what we think we deserve. The pope raised the host, the people bowed their heads, Brigid wondered if that was her period starting now. The people filed in straight lines to get communion, some shuffling, some stamping, as they edged their way confidently towards heaven. Brigid shivered in a flash of cold.

People had started opening their flasks in the park by the time Macartan and Brigid reached the gate. CLOSED DUE TO THE POPE'S VISIT. They said nothing, just caught each other's hands tight and started looking for an opening in the hedge. They climbed through a slit in the ditch and jumped onto the hard ground. Macartan felt as if his hip bones had been pushed up to his ribs with the impact.

The people sang and swayed: 'He's got the whole world in his hands.' (Eleven years later, when some of the poison was leaving, a few people sang 'She's got the whole world in her hands' to Mary Robinson as she drove through the park gates. They giggled low down, knowing where they'd heard it last.) Macartan and Brigid reached the stone wall. Brigid caught Macartan's face and stuck her tongue down his throat. Across the city they had just left, odd souls longed for the comfort of a warm body, the big crook of an arm to bury their faces in, a chest to lie on, a mouth to kiss, anything to take their minds off it.

Brigid and Macartan went into town that night to have a drink. It was the worst thing they could have done for their hearts, because they met too many people who had gone to the park, people they expected more from, were surprised at, and there was a strange sound or was it a smell lurking in the shadows. The streets were full of rubbish, as if an army had trampled through today and left a wash after it. If that was so, Brigid and Macartan were swimming precariously on the edge of it, being watched by the backs of the people on deck. They met Padhraig and Jacinta, who were now furious with themselves for not having gone painting. They had spent the day sitting on a bed together, but they didn't get into it because Padhraig was gay, much to Jacinta's disappointment, not always, but on this day! They waved home-made flags at the screen and shouted, 'Up the pole. Up the pole.'

They all had a drink. The four of them whispered together, hoping to draw some consolation from each other, but it didn't feel enough.

At the airport, Sheena, Brigid, Padhraig and Jacinta hung around while Macartan's parents went through the emotions. Macartan's mother was furious with grief. She would wait six months or more before sending him postcards of the west, of pubs in the west, of musical instruments under blue skies, of valleys pinpointed by intimate rivers and lakes in the west. She would wait. Brigid couldn't kiss him properly, his parents didn't turn their heads for long enough. In the toilet Sheena and Brigid decided to go out together painting once more. Why? There was no need. It must have been the airport, the sense of people fleeing. It must have been. They didn't tell Padhraig or Jacinta – it was too serious.

They drove to the park in the early darkness and painted IF MEN GOT PREGNANT CONTRACEPTION AND ABORTION WOULD BE SACRAMENTS on the monument built for the pope's visit. There were lots of letters. Brigid did fifty of them, hers looked sudden and fluid. Sheena's seven were non-runny and perfect. In the paper the next day you could tell there had been two people. The worst part of it all was doing what Sheena said they had to do afterwards – go to the nearest pub, pee on their hands, and then wash them under the tap. The worst, but she was right. It got rid of the paint from around their fingernails. Sheena then told Brigid that she, too, was emigrating. Brigid said , 'Aw God no', missing her like death already.

Brigid got caught painting a harmless slogan seven years later, one year after the passing of the statute of limitations.

'It may be a harmless slogan, your honour, but the vandalism of the papal cross in the park wasn't.'

The judge's eyes widened into white. 'Six months,' he said.

I got caught. I had a standby job taking in the lottery ticket money in my local shop any time the lottery reached seven hundred thousand pounds or more. A customer left half the receipt one night. The winning numbers were marked on it. Not knowing (I should have) which receipt was needed to claim a prize, I chanced my arm and brought the docket in. By an odd coincidence a hundred pounds went missing from the till the same week. Not me, I wouldn't have the nerve.

'A hundred pounds may not be a lot of money, your honour, but attempting to procure fraudulently eight hundred and sixty thousand, two hundred and ninety-two pounds is.'

'Six months,' he said.

We're getting out next week and Diarmuid is throwing a party for us.

THE BOY FROM DINGWALL

Aodheen got on a train in Inverness because there was nothing left to do but go home after her week's holiday. She was full up with friendship, more than happy, like a cherry tree in blossom, so delighted with itself. More than happy. She was a good candidate for that kind of joy, it was reputed that her father had swum a river every night for a year to meet her mother before they got married.

Aodheen watched passengers getting on. She hoped without much hope that not one of them would sit beside her. A man aged sixty or so stood on the platform with three boys. One of them was getting on the train. Which one? As the whistle blew a fair-haired one stepped out. He may have shaken hands with his father and the two other boys, he certainly didn't kiss or hug any of them. This was the person who sat down opposite Aodheen.

'Is there anyone sitting here?'

She could have said smart-assedly, not that I can see anyway, but that would have given him an opening.

'No,' she said curtly, but warmly enough, because she was, after all, still happy. If only he wouldn't talk.

He had pimples, not too many, not so many to make his face a disaster. His hair was short, he was neither good-looking nor not. He had a contented demeanour. It was not as if he'd ever had to wonder would there be enough left in the pot to cure his hunger or if the school lunch

73

would be edible.

Aodheen looked out the window, more to prevent speech than to take in the hills, the mist with sheep dipping in and out of it like stars on a stage set, the expanse of determined shape between huge mountains, as senseless as an empty dream. She sometimes hated scenery, it made her feel so short-lived, but all the same she was drawn back to it again the way you would be if you had a chance to see, unobserved, two people making love.

The boy sighed. Aodheen ignored it. But he said, plunging into ice cold water, 'I hate going back.'

His youth makes him need to talk, Aodheen thought, and she said, 'What do you work at?' as if answering her would help him. It was the least she could do.

'I'm in the navy,' he said.

Aw Jesus Christ, she said to herself, taking a quick look across her shoulder to see if there were any empty seats. There weren't. Jesus Christ, she thought, how did this happen to me? At the end of such a lovely week too? I wonder, when will he be getting off? Where would you go from Inverness if you were in the navy? Not Edinburgh surely? Surely not?

'Where are you going?'

'We're based in Campbeltown.'

She didn't give a damn where he was based, just where he was going.

'And where do you change trains to get to Campbeltown?'

'Perth.'

'How far away is that?'

'An hour, two hours maybe, I don't know, then I get to

Glasgow, then Campbeltown and I'll be back on the ship about ten.'

Perth, two hours away.

Aodheen looked out the window, again trying to block out what she was thinking. There was nothing to see except a cloud, so low it was nearly touching the ground.

'Would you like a sandwich?' he asked.

'No thanks,' she said, knowing damn rightly that his father and mother were delighted to see him fixed up and off the streets of Dingwall.

Aodheen thought of the Sunday customs in Scotland: if I order wine and they don't serve it on the Sabbath, I'll feel worse than a sinner, but if they do have it, I'll feel much better. They had, which surprised her. The navy boy had Coke.

It was a mistake to get the wine, it thinned out the four feet of air that hung between them, diluted it with drops of red liquid that trickled down her throat and into the atmosphere. He sighed again. The sigh this time was harder to ignore because of the thin air.

'I got engaged at the weekend, that's why I hate going back.'

He'd got engaged to Karen from Culbokie. She was twenty, he was nineteen. His heart, God help him, was flailing about the place with missing her.

'Why don't you get some work around Culbokie, on a farm, or in a shop, or on an oil rig even? That way you'd be near Karen and you wouldn't be in the navy.'

He wasn't listening.

'At least she'll wait now,' the boy said.

Now, how does he figure that out? a ring, a promise, an intention, never delayed anyone if they had somewhere to go. Maybe Karen hadn't, well, in that case she would have waited anyway. Better not tell him that.

'I don't know why I'm so upset leaving her this time.' He wouldn't see her again until Hogmanay. 'I don't know why.'

He should have known that expressing the intention meant a room or rooms that would be theirs, a bed together, winter evenings warmed up. He did really but couldn't put a name on it. That's why he missed her so much this time.

'Surely you could get a job in Inverness even, painting and decorating or something like that?'

'I'll have to run to get the Glasgow train if this one doesn't make up some time. If I was off tonight, I could have a drink when I got there. Three tins on a night off is allowed. I've brought my stereo with me this time.'

He would be able to play music that reminded him of Karen. He was waiting for a sub.

'What does that mean?'

'Waiting for my turn to go down on a sub to learn how to handle one.'

'I see.'

His turn should be coming soon. All those horrible sneaky ships under the water all the time, like peeping toms.

'Why don't you join the fire brigade? That would be exciting,' Aodheen said.

'You could get killed in the fire brigade. More men get killed in the fire brigade than in the navy.'

She was sure that couldn't be right, absolutely certain,

76

but there was little point in pursuing it. This boy was in the navy to stay. At least England didn't have its navy in Ireland with this Scottish boy in it, or did it? The train was only at Pitlochry.

'Are you sure you don't want a sandwich?'

'Oh, all right,' she said doubtfully, as if saying yes to a dangerous thing.

'Egg and onion or cheese?'

So Aodheen ate the egg and onion sandwich made by the mother of the boy in order to help him on his journey to Perth to the train to Glasgow to the train to Campbeltown to his boat, where maybe, chance of all beautiful chances, a sub might be waiting for him.

'Look at the oxbow lake,' he said.

She had never been any good at geology.

'You seem to have an interest in the land,' she said, and then let it peter out.

The boy then wondered out loud if maybe he should join the army if there was a long delay on the sub. There was quicker promotion too. Aodheen thought, well, if you do bucko and end up defending London in Armagh, keep your hands off my lovely man. Her lovely man who lived in Annaghananny and came to Dublin at weekends to see her. Her lovely man with his long legs and his skittery laugh. Last year he went home to Annaghananny one Sunday evening. He was stopped on the way. A man with no face put him up against the wall.

''Avin't seen you 'round 'ere before.'

'Haven't fucking seen too much of you either,' her man muttered to the wall, which was nearly in his mouth by now.

'Wot did you say?'

'Nothing.'

'Wot do you werk at, den?' the man with no face said.

'I'm a graphic artist.'

'Ah, me sister's a graphic awtist,' the man said chattily, adjusting the gun to lean it against the next rib so he could run his hand down the inside of Aodheen's man's leg.

'Me sister's a graphic awtist back at 'ome. She'd luv t'werk 'ere – not *'ere* – in Dublin, she wouldn't werk *'ere*. D'you think she cud get sumfink?'

Aodheen's man wasn't sure about that.

'OK you can go.'

And he went, as meekly as a lamb, the taste of whitewash on his tongue, a spot on his ribs blazing warm where the gun had poked into him.

'Join the army!' Her voice pitched itself wildly across the four feet. 'And kill the Irish!' It kicked out of her, hard, unforgiving, like a box in the mouth, and that wasn't like her.

'They kill us.'

'Not if you weren't there, they wouldn't,' she said, really not wanting to talk about it any more. Suppose he went mad and caught her by the throat, suppose he didn't but there were others listening who did. Suppose. But the boy didn't know what was good for him.

'What do you think about the terrorists?' he asked only a little uncertainly.

'Which ones?' she said.

'What do you mean?' he said.

And she didn't spare him, the poor little boy from Dingwall who had got engaged to Karen from Culbokie at the weekend.

Aodheen's man told her that his Scottish friends had come over once. They visited him only because they thought Armagh was in the South. They couldn't with all honesty discuss politics because they knew that their neighbours' sons and their own cousins, indeed, were pointing guns all over the joint. It upset them but they couldn't very well admit it. Every time they got stopped her man said to himself, goody (which was not normal), particularly if the soldiers were Scottish, that'll put the wind up them, maybe they'll go home now and tell the truth.

Aodheen and he (well he started it) laughed their heads off one time when they saw a helicopter dropping supplies into an army base on the border. They couldn't use the road or they might be blown up. They saw parcels being dropped.

'Tinned beans,' he chortled.

And then they saw a jeep being dropped. It was hilarious, it looked as if the jeep was flying through the air.

'Oh dear,' her man said, wiping the tears from his eyes. 'Oh dear. God that's gas.'

The first time she went to Armagh to meet her lovely man they ate dinner in Drumsill House Hotel, a house with as much glass as wall, that looks out on placid landscape. They dreamed into the quiet, staring at horses, stray ducks and peacocks. The men that burst on to their picture looked at first like frantic turkeys but then she saw the guns and saw them jooking up on hedges.

'What are they doing here?' she said, not so much from ignorance as from surpise.

'Aw, just prancin' about so we'll see them and some of us will finally lose the head and take a shot at them, then they can catch us, put us in jail, so there's reason for someone else to take a shot at them. Provocation it's called,' he said.

That was the first time she noticed just how skittery his laugh was. No, she didn't spare the navy boy.

'Aw, I don't think I would join the army really,' he said.

The boy had sent away games one time, board games that he had made up himself. He had sent them to a few companies but they had sent them back.

'Maybe you could get a job in a toy shop. Then you could get toys cheap when you and Karen have children.'

It was the 'when' that made him go scarlet.

'I'll get a sub soon,' he said.

In time Perth came up the way birthdays do, or your turn to have a sleep-in does, or the way the sun lights up.

'Don't forget your stereo,' she said.

He bundled all his stuff together, said goodbye, he'd see her maybe if ever he was in Ireland – Aodheen smiled at that – and he rushed out to get his train to Glasgow.

She pulled the window down and leaned out, trying once again. 'Join the fire brigade,' she yelled after him, not knowing why she wanted to save him in particular. Still, she supposed if he stuck to subs, he mightn't do anyone any harm in peacetime.

Three weeks later he got his first go. He did something wrong (it wasn't his fault) and pulled a fishing boat with three men in it to the very bottom of the sea. It's still there and the navy hasn't made up its mind yet what to do with him.

BIRTH CERTIFICATES

'Call me Regina. There's nothing so daft-sounding as Miss Clarke. Some like Mrs, but Miss is stretching it, I always think,' Miss Clarke, Miss Regina Clarke, said to Maolíosa, shaking her hand heartily.

It's like as if she's shaking hands from her nipple out, thought Maolíosa, at the same moment also thinking, what a ridiculous thing to imagine. What made me think of that?

'Sit down. No here, this seat is more comfortable.'

Maolíosa sat on the edge of it. Regina had a bosom that an eleven-year-old would be absolutely sure to get a peep at. Certainly you should be able to see some of it, say from underneath the short summer sleeve, if she lifted one of her arms up, or definitely if she bent over to get something. God, what's got into me? Maolíosa wondered. Yesterday she had told a friend about a desperate craving for chocolate that had come over her recently.

'No I'm not, I'm not,' she said, annoyed at her friend's eyebrow which had shrivelled up into a question mark. 'It's the spring, the summer, the sunshine, eating chocolate gives you a rush, a whoomph, like sex, we need it in the first flush of sun.'

'People know so much about themselves these days it takes the fun out of it.'

The room from where Miss Clarke worked was heavily wooden. The books and the old papers that were scattered on her desk had established their own smell. It had got into her, this smell of forever written descriptions of people's lives. The shelves were dark wood too. It was only this, the dark wood in the shelves, that saved the room from being the dispensary where Maolíosa had got her injections when she was a child. Come to think of it, Miss Clarke could have been the nurse, although you wouldn't be inclined to think about nipples if you were getting an injection.

'I just wanted to know how you started,' Maolíosa said.

'Well, I am prepared to discuss that, and that sort of thing, but nothing else really, because there are too many confidences at risk.'

'I understand that, Miss Clarke.'

'Regina.'

'Regina.'

'What's your name again?'

'Maolíosa.'

'Well, Maolíosa, I never wanted to start and although I've done this thing now for twenty-five years, mostly in my own time, I've never been paid a penny. But I don't mind. It was Jennifer really. She kept at me so much – surely I must be able to find out who her mother was – it's not possible that all trace of the original birth certs can't be found, surely it would do no harm, surely as a trusted employee I could get the birth certs, surely I must know after all these years how much she wanted to see her once, just once. And in the end I thought, well, I'll try, just to see for myself if I could find someone's mother, and a year later when I found her I thought, what harm could it do? What harm? So I went to her, Jennifer's mother, and she agreed, so for Jennifer's

thirtieth birthday present I introduced her to her mother.
I suppose the word spread after that. There's a country full
of them out there, and more again, much more again, outside the country. They mostly come from England now. But
I don't meet those ones, they usually know the address by
then, unless, of course, the mother has asked me from this
end, which is even dicier. Ah yes. Even dicier.'

Miss Clarke shuffled the papers.

'Ah yes, sometimes it can be very frightening. You know,
I've done a year or whatever of work and then they're meeting, having tea somewhere, and I'm at home wondering
what would happen if it all went wrong, if they killed each
other or something. I find myself always uneasy when
there's a first meeting on. Then, if one of them doesn't want
to meet again and one does, I sometimes think they might
kill me, for the address. Would you like a cup of tea?'

They had a cup of tea. Maolíosa spun yarns to herself
about how the editor would love this story. She saw promotion, even heard voices saying, ask Maolíosa, she'd probably have some ideas on that.

She went home knowing approximately how many people
had contacted Miss Clarke since the day the word got out
that she had found someone's mother. She knew how many
were male and female, what their general motivation was,
how Miss Clarke went about looking for their mothers. Miss
Clarke always stressed that, first, the mother might be impossible to find, second, she might not want to meet them
(usually for fear of her husband), third, she might be dead.
If she found the mother and the mother was agreeable, Miss
Clarke set up a meeting, after much advice to both not to

expect too much and not to whatever else was appropriate in the individual case. You want to see some of the mothers that were mothers of some of the people she met. It would make the hairs stand on your head.

The room had got less like a dispensary as Miss Clarke talked. Maolíosa had jotted down notes on scraps of paper, one case was even written on her hand. She had been reluctant to write too much or to take out a formal notebook because Miss Clarke eyed the pen and paper suspiciously. But she would sort it out now, spread mingy sentences on the desk and reshape them to give paper readers a sparse undemanding picture of some thousands of secrets.

Cathal came home at twenty past five on the dot as usual. He was also supportive. In fact, he was god-damned nearly perfect. (Life must have been easy for him, thought Maolíosa, because she was driven to having some defence against his perfection.) She herself spent a lot of her time being irritable, being unsatisfied, being unreasonable. But life couldn't have been that easy for him. His parents had died five years ago, just before Maolíosa met him. He had no family, none at all. Surely that was hard, Maolíosa thought.

'She's really an interesting woman. Very unselfish. All that work for no money, no recognition. She can't even really tell anyone because in a sense it's breaking the spirit of adoption.'

'Perhaps she sees it as a hobby, your Miss Clarke.' He had taken an extraordinary dislike to Miss Clarke, he who never disliked anyone.

'Oh! Forget it, it doesn't really matter,' Maolíosa said,

thinking that she might ruin the evening. He was entitled to his opinion. 'The article should be good anyway, although she won't let me meet any of the people concerned. Naturally, I suppose.'

'Your articles usually are. Probably a lot of unnecessary trouble though.'

'How did you get on today?' she thought it best to say.

And so they passed the evening, like any other, mostly in a pleasant way, a way founded on steadiness. The embarrassing, scarcely believable gymnastics of their first year were now an unshared memory that served only to prove, surely, their compatibility. Maolíosa supposed it was love that wove its way in and out between their sentences, their agreements, their apologies after their disagreements.

Sometimes Maolíosa looked at Cathal, like now, and noticed different things about him. Look – his moustache, it leaned to one side of his face as if it were a wind-beaten hedge, she'd never noticed that before. It was nice to know that there were new things. Oh Cathal, she thought, if we were younger we could be brother and sister and I would help you do your homework; here give me that, I'll do it for you, I've finished my own. Thanks. And then we'd grow up. I could leave, you wouldn't mind and I wouldn't mind, and you'd be there if I needed you.

Regina Clarke listened to the radio as she soaked in the bathroom. Tonight she was going out with her younger, ten years younger, brother. They had a proper night out once a month, not just because they were brother and sister but because they liked each other, enjoyed a lot of the same outings, could watch the embarrassing parts of the films as if they were either the most natural thing, so much so that they didn't deserve unease, or else so unnatural as to cause them no bother, because that carry-on couldn't be for real. He was a relief from herself at times, a light-hearted un-worried person. Regina generally got through her days with a minimum of panic, but sometimes that job! Not her real job, the other one. Each attempted finding was a challenge, she could always cope with one expectant person, but when her trail was getting hot, and then hotter, she began to worry. Two people, now, linked through her – well, linked would be the wrong word, they were, after all, mother and child – dependent on her, to say yes or no way, no way, never. How will she tell that to another one?

'Your mother, taking all things into consideration, would prefer not . . . .'

'I don't believe you, I don't believe you, you've led me on.'

She put more hot water in the bath, slid herself forward and soaked her head. Her thick brown curls straightened, her hair swam as if it had a life of its own, spread out like her heart did sometimes. Her heart which didn't always live the life that other people thought it was undergoing.

She could hear people whispering that she never married, some with sympathy coated with curiosity, but when she said it herself, 'I never married', it sounded more like an underground triumph. Once, she had been very taken over with a man. Lots of times, still, she was taken over for a few tipsy days. But nowadays her patience ran out of gusto and the tipsy days ran into hangovers before a week was past.

That man was a different story. It was twenty-five years ago. He had spent a number of years in America and so had acquired a certain amount of mystery and an even greater amount of warranted or unwarranted confidence – how were any of them to know what he had actually achieved out there? He had black hair, was born in Galway, and never told the whole truth. As soon as he was sure of her, which only took a few months, he flirted continuously. On the edge of her mind, she could feel the indignity of it. His flirting, always in company where she could be made to feel small, was like a wasp buzzing around near her ear, although she tried not to look as she swatted annoyance from her face.

One day he just flirted himself away. Her friends said afterwards she was 'far too good for him', but she never really minded him or the memory of him. These same friends fell into marriage one by one. Regina had watched just-married and about-to-be-married women converge around the latest ring – isn't it lovely, let me see, it's beautiful. She felt obscenity escaping in puffs from inside that circle. She could never crowd around a ring. The ones who had most adamantly complained about other new wives losing contact with their friends were the very ones who hid themselves in cupboards after their nuptials. 'God help them,' said Regina, when she thought about them, and got on with her job and her second job.

Some evenings when Regina was soaking she imagined her bath much bigger than it was, ten times larger at least, and there the important things of her life swam with her – a job well done; brisk Saturday mornings in the city

87

turning languid, holding her there until afternoon; dinners; absolutely special words from men whom she had the nerve to leave; music evenings with her brother; her fine face. And the annoyances swam away.

Today she didn't do that because she must go out. The young woman who came was nice. She was coming again next week. She hurried to meet her brother. She always thought of him as her brother, not as Martin.

'No,' the editor said, 'it's not of sufficient interest.'

'That's not true,' Maolíosa said.

The editor had important diplomacies to consider, a story like that could upset a lot of people from all sides – his assistant editor, for instance, had an adopted child, this much he knew for definite. He was sure Maolíosa would question the morality of adoption in the surprised way she had. Sometimes he couldn't decide, and didn't really want to find out, if her surprise was genuine. She was good, but didn't understand words like 'necessity' or 'arrangement' or 'best suit'. How do you think his assistant editor would react? And who else was there in the office? You never knew. Why, you were never even sure about yourself. Maolíosa left early. She stepped out into a shockingly spring day.

I will do it. I will do it. So! So what if this stinking pompous fart doesn't want it. So what. She sighed because really she knew that all that rage blowing up like a balloon was simply an empty reassurance that she was getting somewhere in her job. And it was empty. Nothing ever came out on a page in that paper but the briefest glimpse of the truth. But I will do it, she thought, one whole story, or maybe small parts of several stories. I will write it down for a start.

She said to Cathal, exactly as he came in the door: 'Guess what? he won't even contemplate it.'

'Someone has sense.'

'I'm going to do something anyway. I feel a certain responsibility to those people.'

'That's nonsense. You don't even know any of them. It would suit you better to have responsibility to people you do know.'

'Oh well, it won't do any harm.'

'You think,' he said.

So when Maolíosa called to see Regina the following week it was with a different proposition.

'Let me meet some of the people or at least tell me some of the stories and I'll promise to keep their identities secret.'

'But what for?'

'I want to write a play maybe.' The idea of a play had only just struck her but it might be one way. 'With you as the central character.'

Regina Clarke smiled an altogether amused smile and yet a line pulled at her left eye. 'Ah, no.'

'But . . . '

Maolíosa was determined. She had been awake since dawn, plotting the truth, enjoying the excitement of it. (Pity about Cathal's inexplicable antipathy.) She had planned the exposure of the real story, not the signing of the papers that complied with an act drawn up by a government – no, the real stories.

She cajoled Miss Clarke into daydreaming. Miss Clarke dreamt real worth into her life. Because she was engaged with such dynamite emotions – deciding to find your mother was hardly like buying a house – she sometimes had to believe that everyone else's life was such a trivial thing really. That way she could approach each search as if it didn't make a blind bit of difference whether or not this person ever met its mother. If she didn't do this, then they might all crack up under the nerves. But if everyone else's life, mother, was a trivial matter, your own wasn't – it was, well, it was life. Yours. Your one and only.

To tell or not to tell? She'd spent her life with these secrets, gone to bed with them, even forgotten some of them. But surely she did deserve something out of it. Truly her part in it was worth something. She had managed to calm people as they plunged through dangerous thoughts, she had even understood them – didn't she know that deciding to find your mother was hardly like buying a house? The government had never paid her, even though it helped them that she was doing this, took the pressure off them, so to speak, no one had ever paid her. Still, if she did tell, if she hinted a do-it-yourself find-your-mother method, then you might have hordes of people looking for their mothers, people turning up after Sunday dinner on unsuspecting doorsteps, mothers who were just about to take a nap saying, wait there a minute, nearly closing the door (you couldn't completely close the door on your own flesh and blood if they were actually standing there in front of you, rather than lying in a cot) and saying John, or Peter, or Paddy, or Mick, could you come here for a minute there's something I have to tell you. The lucky ones would at least have a separate sitting room in which to drop the bombshell.

Could she tell her life story without dropping DIY hints? Maolíosa talked on, piling up reasons why she should, and if they did it in some way different than a newspaper, they could have more scope, they could mix the names up. Colours of hair, hospitals, counties of origin, birth weight, could all be swapped around.

It was the sound of Maolíosa's voice that did the trick, Miss Clarke had to say to herself afterwards, because suddenly a certain mischief took her over and shook her like you would a thing you wanted to put life into and she said, 'Why not, what harm could it do?'

And so the next six months were spent delving in and out of stories. Sometimes in Regina's office, overlooking the canal and the ducks.

'What do you mean the mother was married when she had it? But I thought . . . '

Maolíosa was confident here now. Once, when sitting on the desk, she caught herself staring at Regina's V-necked dress. That thing they call a cleavage – it was like a crease, a watershed, the down shape of any single thing thrown in a heap – why was it so breathtaking? It was as if that line was the piercing needle of the body below. Had Miss Clarke had many, any, orgasms? Regina was judging her this evening, she was sure. Sometimes she was friendly, but sometimes she looked down her nose at Maolíosa, bragging years. Maolíosa was still young enough to hate that. Did Miss Clarke have many orgasms? Maolíosa rubbed her ankle against the desk leg to bring back the conversation they'd been having. What business of hers was it anyway?

Other times they met in Regina's house. It was a severe

91

semi-detached house, one of those places that could never have been part of anybody's plan, how could it? A blank, faceless transfer, that might crop up in a nightmare somewhere. Everyone on the street was married, except Regina. The husbands all earned the same money, the wives had all stopped work at the same time, done pre-natal classes together, decided there was no need for their husbands to be there when the births would happen (that way they could have an extra day's holiday when the wives would be able to enjoy their company), discussed birth control, and had second children within three months of each other. Regina's brother had seen the house on his way home from work. They went to see it together. When they turned into the street, Regina gasped, 'What are you trying to do to me? A street like this! You'd have me out here surrounded by Mr and Mrs, people washing cars and mowing lawns.'

But inside, the house was different, different enough to show how even more different it could be. And now it was. For such a young and correct house, it held the old furniture, the strewn records, the dust, with unexpected style. It had made the bathroom its own, the enormous bath, the foams, the smells. The bathroom jolted Maolíosa, the first time. It was such a warm, well, warm and wet, bathroom that she was embarrassed. Imagine Miss Clarke. Ah! Just imagine.

And then when Cathal wasn't there they met in Maolíosa's flat, one window of which looked out on other windows and a series of scorched gardens. Regina liked the austerity of the few unmatched pieces of furniture. Maolíosa and Cathal never accumulated enough money to get a set of anything, not even of cups.

In these three places, with their different furnitures, their different views, Maolíosa and Regina began to write down the facts. But first the stories, and some of them Maolíosa would have to meet herself. Regina would tell her who she could meet, fix it up in some pleasant place. All part of their adventure. Where there were no proven words, Maolíosa imagined sentences, conversations, between the pregnant women and the men.

THE MEEK
'The band was good.'
   He wasn't sure: 'From where we were you couldn't see them.'
   'Frank, I'm going to have a baby.'
   'Jesus Christ.'

THE EXPECTING THE WORST
'Could I speak to Mr Hogan, please?'
   'May I ask who is calling?'
   'It's personal.'
   'Eamon, I have to tell you now, it's easier by telephone, I'm pregnant.'
   'Jesus Christ.'

THE JAUNTY AND CONFIDENT
'Guess what?'
   'What?'
   'We're going to have a baby.'
   'Jesus Christ.'

THE TERRIFIED
'They'll kill me. I'm pregnant.'
  'Jesus Christ.'

Yes, Jesus Christ. The country was a garden full of virgin births. And then there were the blanks where no conversation had taken place at all because there was no point, or she knew the answer anyway and wouldn't humiliate herself further, or she was too embarrassed because she didn't know him well enough, or this would be his excuse to force a wedding on her and in no time she'd be up to her neck in muck and his life.

  Maolíosa and Regina lifted their sadness sometimes by concentrating on the mischief they were doing. They were blowing bits out of the bottom of the rock.

'No, I don't want her to find me. How could I look her in the eye? I abandoned her. I hope she's been happy and that they were good to her. Why? Why did I do it? Because, because I was told to, that's why. My parents are now in heaven, no doubt, with the rest of them.'

  The woman's eyes were hollow. She was tall and see-through thin. She wore her tailored, expensive clothes easily, because she was used to them all her life but she didn't get any comfort from such good material. The clothes themselves would have given the world to be worn with delight.

  'Actually I do want her to find me, maybe she would forgive me.'

Aoife had changed her name to Eva, it sounded more

important. She was tall and happily thin. She didn't care beyond the next customer in the nightclub, the next good-looking customer that is. She was going to London next week, where you can get jobs like these in the *daytime*, all day long – winebars. Winebars everywhere. Two of her friends from the orphanage were already there (there had never been any 'they' to be good to her). One of them was getting her a job. No, she didn't care whether or not she ever saw her mother, she knew others that had done it and it wasn't *good* for them. Much too risky meeting your mother, you wouldn't know *what* she'd be like. She could be any one of a thousand kinds of person, Eva knew all the types that came to nightclubs, and you mightn't like *anything* about her. It would be nice, though, if she was *stinking* rich, but there was no guarantee that she'd give any of it to *her*, so far, she hadn't actually fallen about the place proving how much she loved her. No, it wouldn't be a good idea – one of her friends went to see her mother and the biggest shock was that there were three children who looked *exactly*, I mean *exactly*, like herself. So did the mother. It was spooky, her not being used to seeing people that looked in any way like her. I *tell* you, it was spooky. No, she was going to London next week so she wouldn't have time anyway.

Maolíosa dreamed about the two of them. She couldn't bear that she knew something they didn't know. The dream choked in her mouth, making it smell of vomit. But in the morning she forced herself to accept that they had no daily worries about the matter. The mother had a simple ever-lasting unattainable desire to be forgiven but she didn't think about it all the time. It was just there, like a medium bad backache. And even if her daughter did forgive her, it would still be there. The daughter had no desire whatever to have her curiosity stirred up. She had grown up with her peers. Old people, like mothers, weren't that important, they had always had nuns. The last thing mother and child needed was Maolíosa with her caring and her bloody good will.

Regina said, oh, that's nothing. But she knew how Maolíosa felt. She'd get immune though, just like undertakers do. Presumably the first funeral was always the worst. She was also afraid, because if Maolíosa started pointing out these things, would it not remind her of each and every case? How many times had she looked out at that canal? They always sat down for a few minutes before they came in to her. Naturally, she supposed, it was a big step. They always stared at the ducks. Young women, young men, middle-aged women. One middle-aged woman, middle of what age? Regina remembered her. She had looked out the window and saw her staring at the ducks and knew that that must be Mrs Coyle. She had a dark brown scarf with a horse's head on it – a big wide head, big open eyes, and a speck of brown on its forehead. Around the edge of the scarf the smaller horses' heads looked out satisfiedly at passers-by as if it was the most natural place to be. One of the horses' heads was mangled in the knot tied under Mrs Coyle's chin. Another peeped over Mrs Coyle's shoulder and also stared at the ducks.

Mrs Coyle explained: 'Birthdays have always been bad but this one finished me. It didn't go away after the day was over. Every day now is his birthday. I have to do

something.' She was falling in inside, landslides were tear-
ing away from her heart and dropping into her stomach.
His birthday had a hold on her face and was pinching it.
'You have to help me or I will die, I really will die.'

His birthday might kill her. Regina asked her, what about
her husband? as she usually did, but this time she particularly meant it because someone would have to be told
about this poor woman's heart.

'My husband is very good, very kind, oh, he's a wonderful husband.'

'Well, would you not perhaps tell him then?'

Mrs Coyle thought it a pity, considering. Considering
what? Well, she said shyly, when she was having him the
doctor said he'd have to do a section. But there was one
other thing they could do instead of a section and it wouldn't
leave a scar in case she ever got married and didn't want
her husband to know and would she prefer that? and she
said, yes, she would prefer that. They broke her pelvis –
it seemed like they did it with a saw – a hammer or a saw.

Regina bit her lip and involuntarily held on to her pubic
bone the way men grab their balls during a free kick.

Because of going through all that, it had seemed silly to
tell him at first and then a month was a year and a half-truth
became a half-lie and then a year was five years and she
had her 'first' child, and a half-lie became such a monstrous
untruth that it didn't bear thinking about. And now his
birthday had got her.

Regina met Mrs Coyle often in the next six months and
these meetings kept Mrs Coyle from dying. In the end she
told her husband because there didn't seem anything else

she could do because she had stopped sleeping. The pinch went out of her face. He took it like a gentleman but it diminished certainty for him. And yet he got something from the 'announcement', as he henceforth called his wife's squeezed sentences. He had been picked to be one of the men who married women who had secretly had children before their weddings. It did something for him. He then came with Mrs Coyle to see Regina.

Regina found Mrs Coyle's son, a fair-haired young man, who seldom smiled and even when he did his face remained flat. He was delighted. They all met and that should have been the end of that. But one day Mrs Coyle turned up again. She had hurried frantically past the ducks.

'He wants to know who his father is. He's very insistent. Is that normal?'

'Well, does your husband know?'

'He never asked. I suppose he thought it improper. And I never told him, I thought that it would make it too real. You see everything is real, once I've told it to him.'

Regina said that Mrs Coyle would have to decide for herself.

The next day Mrs Coyle stood waiting for the shop to open in her village and decided. It would all have to be told now and she put her hand to her throat. Her husband's boss. His mealy-mouthed, snide, know-all boss. God help us, it would all have to be told now.

Regina felt sorry to have held one over on Maolíosa.

'I didn't really mean that it was nothing,' she said. 'Here, do you need any carpet? Remember the man I told you about last week? he's just met his mother, he's forty-five, well, his friend works on the ships, maintaining them, and apparently they often remove all the carpet from the ships even though only some of it is worn and he said that if ever I wanted any to give him a shout. It is always the one colour, red, blue or green.'

'Oh great, we certainly could do with a carpet.'

They needed more than a new carpet, Maolíosa thought.

There had been an awful row. Maolíosa still had a headache. She had come home. She had smiled at Cathal and then told him about the woman she'd met, an acquaintance of Regina's brother, who wanted to help, because she had never quite recovered from her brush with 'that kind of thing'. Maolíosa knew that Cathal hated these interviews but she didn't know the seriousness of why. Anyway, she had to tell someone. The woman today wondered what life was like now for the woman who had been in the bed beside her.

'I remember she told me that she was an alcoholic. I said that she couldn't be, not at nineteen, but then the visitors came from AA so she must have been. She said she never remembered getting pregnant – maybe she did but couldn't admit it. She was giving the baby up. Up to where? I used to think as we both lay, trying not to disturb our stitches. "They say if I keep it I'll only go back on the drink." "Who are they?" "The friends from AA and my mother" (who had come sneakily on her own, supposedly going for a check on her varicose veins, and never looked at the child once). "They say! They say! But what do you say, Linda, what do you say?" "Well, I know one thing, I'm not taking it out of that basket. It's not fair to expect me to do anything with it. I'm giving it up, amn't I? The nurses can change its nappy." And I began to feel privileged to wash the shit from around my baby's bottom. I put my nipple into my baby's mouth, touching his cheek with it first so he snuggled his mouth round and open, burying his nose in my breast.

'My baby drank guilt, as I could see from the corner of my eye Linda's basket untouched, writhing instead of rocking between the bedposts where it was hung, sending screeches up and up, its mother with stone for a face, and then a nurse would come. "Now Linda," she would say, "you know it's best if you get to know it. Then you won't feel later that you had no choice." "I'm not touching that basket." And there I was, allowed to feed my baby with my very own nipple because I could take it home because a man had asked me to marry him and I had said yes, or maybe I had asked him. Think of anything, I whispered to my baby as inconspicuously as I could manage. When Linda left the ward I always picked him up and squeezed him properly and then I would go to Linda's basket where I would lay my fingers on her child's head and say some tight useless cliché.

'Forty-eight hours after Linda and I had pushed our babies out, I turned on my left side and saw her move towards her basket. She leaned up on her hunkers, then thought better of it, moved again, then back. There was a god playing with her to see how much magnet she was. She got down from the bed carefully and pulled herself ghostlike to the basket. She dug her hands into it, clenching her eyes, and came out with a baby. She seemed surprised at it, then kissed it full on the mouth. I heard her whisper as if the words were escaping from her. So from then on my baby drank tears and apprehension because Linda would not leave her baby out of her arms even when the nurses said, "Come on now, it needs to sleep; come on, you need to sleep." "I can sleep all I like later," she said.

'I asked to be let out a few hours early because I hadn't the stomach to watch the passing over of Linda's baby to an intermediary, who would then pass it over to some married infertile couple. That's how I came to leave the hospital on a Sunday morning instead of a Sunday evening.'

When Maolíosa told Cathal what the woman had said, there had been the terrible row. Cathal had been like a mad man. And Maolíosa, after she had cried away all her rage at him, gave up the interviews, the talks and Regina.

The news came on, Maolíosa and Cathal smiled at each other. They didn't always look at each other over breakfast but when they caught each other's eyes on the way up for more toast, or on the way down to drink more tea, they smiled. A smile that had everlasting written on it because if, as well as being totally loyal, they could do for each other and themselves what they had done last night, with the covers thrown back, then everlasting must surely be on the cards. The news reader said: 'The new Children's Bill which does away with the status of illegitimacy comes before the Dáil today. There will be no more Nobody's Child.'

'Christ,' Maolíosa said, 'they never *were* nobody's child, they were their mothers' children, surely.'

But Cathal turned off the radio. A flash, like the snarl of

a dog, passed over his lips and eyes but there he now was, smiling again. Maolíosa would have to split herself a little. Last nights should be better nurtured. They should have put music on, not the news. Her headache was back. And the row started again. 'I've given up doing the interviews, what more do you want?' The day was ruined.

Cathal imagined himself running into a river and forgetting how to swim. He could leave, couldn't he? But he couldn't leave all this. This for him was the whole of it. Cooked breakfasts in bed on Saturday mornings, someone to talk to in the evening, every evening, the sound of her feet in bedroom slippers dragging as in a slow dance around the kitchen, when it was her turn to cook breakfast on a Saturday morning. This was the plug that stopped a deluge from falling on his head. But now he was dreaming every night that a river was coming towards him from the other direction. Yet last night he had woken in a cold sweat and found himself lying peacefully. The front of his right foot lay curled on the back of her left foot for all the world like a lover who had decided.

Maolíosa put order on the shelves, the toilet, the bedclothes. She walked out, pleased with such tidiness. In the bank she noticed a man whom she'd last noticed two years ago. He had got older, got settled. She remembered him as a young boy. He looked over all the bank now with confidence – when she first noticed him he had kept his eyes down and only looked at a desk or another clerk when he was standing right beside it or them. He seemed to be growing into the bank, he even had the nerve now to wear a slightly creased shirt. How could anyone be expected to spend their life on that one side of a counter, being stared at mechanically by customers? Were they very nice to him when he had a hangover? He must have hangovers, he now had a drink belly. So clean, God they were all so clean. They had to wash the smell of sex off themselves every morning – you couldn't have them smelling like that in a bank and especially not when the desks were so near each other and the canteen was so small. Pity that – because smelling the smell next morning was often the best part, letting it waft up in the middle of your stomach and through the nose to your brain, which did the remembering, the reconstruction, and made you feel all randy again.

She left the bank, upset by the sight of the young man growing into the bank walls. What was she going to do now? There was a burning above her legs, and an aggravating tic in her brain telling her to leave, leave everything, free herself, spread her wings. It was not good enough to spend your life with one man. Especially when he had become so cantankerous. It was not good enough that she got enormous pleasure from tidying shelves. And yet when her job took her away she thought all the time of her one man. Even more so if she was in bed with somebody else – her eyes filled up with tears at the thought of such simple pleasure. Once a man was the someone else it meant he was new, exciting, took his time, looked at her maybe, worked his way up to her very womb, and grinned with surprise at her lack of inhibition. But what would she do without her one man, what would happen between five and ten in the evening? She would drink too much, go to bed with too many unsuitable men who only needed a tight body to wrap around their

103

pricks in order to make masturbation easier. But then she might also lie down beside a stranger and they might drink each other's very breath, staring deep down to the backs of their eyes, touching their fingers over each other's lips, while they joined the bottom part of their bodies together, pretending that they were doing nothing more that putting two parts of a jigsaw together, until their eyes became dim, misted over, their smiles became a little pained and they devoured each other like wolves, screaming love, sex, betrayal, emptiness, fullness and pleasure, as they kissed each other's cheekbones afterwards. Why did sex make such a different thing of friendship? Oh well, it did, thank God, thank God.

Regina went for a walk. She would meet her brother and his friend at seven. They were to have a meal. She had no curiosity about her brother's friend. She might have had but she was too preoccupied with disappointment. She hadn't believed that Maolíosa would drop the venture so completely. Because she thought Maolíosa stronger than that. That's couples for you, she tried hard not to sneer. She walked over Charlemont Street bridge and looked down on a duck sliding into the water. It gave a back wave of its foot, a dismissive wave, kicking the water away without a ripple. Well, if you're worried, it's your problem, you don't seriously expect me to take on the pain of every fool that stares at me? I'd be dead long ago of worried duck disease if I did that. It gave another wave. Point taken, Regina said, and walked on. Saturday is couples day around Grafton Street, they were everywhere, fighting and kissing. I suppose Maolíosa and Cathal are among them. They won't be fighting now because he got his way. She walked behind a man, woman and child. The man and woman seemed to pursue each other, because although she was a few steps in front of him, her comments seemed to be directed at his back.

'You're as thick as two short planks.'

Regina thought that a funny thing for a woman dressed like her to say.

He said, 'A small zip on your mouth wouldn't go astray.'

She said, 'If you wanted to be an actor, why didn't you join the Abbey?'

He said, 'God preserve me from your ignorance, that's all I ask.'

The child ignored them. It could have slipped away unnoticed. Couples, Regina sniffed, and turned into another street.

Another child was having its day. It said, sure and clear, 'I love the sound of my daddy's voice.'

Regina was startled and turned to look at such a child. That was obviously her daddy. He was beaming. Certainly. Always as soon as Regina had couples relegated they started kissing, even the sedate ones in bristly woollen jumpers. That was her luck with dismissiveness. But really, Maolíosa should have been stronger. After all the work they both had done, not to talk of Regina's whole life, but, of course, Maolíosa was a little young, acted too surprised at times, was too surprised. Acted beaten at times, was beaten.

'That was particularly difficult. The mother had been forced to give it up. It seems the father was a priest,' Regina said.

Maolíosa said, 'If you had published that, there would have been an uproar. An absolute uproar.'

'No, I don't think so. It's not what is uncovered and said openly that matters, it's who says it.'

Maolíosa had looked beaten.

When Regina had explained the procedure for making out the new birth certificate for the adopted child, Maolíosa had said, astonished, 'But that's illegal. Completely illegal. A birth certificate says who your parents are. Well, who you came from. You can't just go and change it. It's illegal.'

'Of course it's illegal,' Regina almost snapped, annoyed at Maolíosa's honest bafflement.

'Birth certificates are a complete insult to mothers anyway. They're all about the fathers,' Maolíosa said.

'That's nothing to do with us.'

Maolíosa had looked both surprised and beaten. She was too young. But so resilient. She would call again when the trouble with Cathal had blown over. Of course she would. Regina had better go home, have her bath, and meet her brother.

Months passed as months will. Other things happened to Regina, Cathal and Maolíosa. They ate, slept, worked, walked, ran for buses, read newspapers. But other things were really just padding. All three had, in different ways, been linked on a roller coaster. They knew that this would not be the end of them, could not be the end of this. Regina waited with patience because she was sure. Other things happened but they weren't important.

*

106

Maolíosa was twiddling her laces, hugging her knees, closing her eyes tight to stop herself from crying. Come on, come on, crying will only be temporary relief, it won't solve anything. Answer the questions, Maolíosa, she said sternly to herself. She had divided them into single questions rather than one big unruly one. What am I going to do? Why is Cathal so impossible? Has he got tired of me? What am I going to do? What would he say if I said I was leaving? And then, in case he'd say, well, all right, she thought, oh don't be silly, I'm not going to say that. Of course I'm staying. I'm staying because I want to stay, he's just out of sorts. It must have been all that talk about children and parents. His own parents were dead, she would have to remind herself of that again. Funny how you could forget the biggest thing about other people's lives just because your own mother was still there somewhere to run to. I'm sorry, Cathal, sorry, but I'll have to make up my mind, for you, for me. Oh I'll stay, my love, I'll stay. Could I let him go? No. But it would surely be better than this recurring politeness that festers into torrents of gall every chance he gets. I could let him go because I'd have to, because he's mine no more than he's anyone else's. I couldn't help him pack, nor could I give him a train or taxi fare, nor kiss him goodbye, nor wish him good luck, but if I had to . . . I couldn't allow myself to think of someone else touching his face, some stranger unbuttoning his shirt, him ringing up a telephone number belonging to some complete and utter drop-in, some pointless nobody, but if I had to . . . I think I will ask him.

But she didn't ask him, as such. She said in a low voice

in reaction to one more sniping hour, 'Either I go or you tell me what's got into you.'

She waited for him to say, well, go then. Instead he looked at her with eyes that were like death. She had not noticed how black they had become. They startled her.

'Because my parents are not dead. I am one of your precious adopted children. I do not know who my parents are. Yes, I was reared by two people who tried to make me believe that it doesn't matter. For that ignorance I hate them and buried them the day I left what they so presumptuously call home.'

He put the kettle on and looked a little amused. He was terribly relieved. The black went from his eyes and soaked into Maolíosa's skin, making her grey.

Maolíosa stayed grey for a week, her hands shook a lot; she felt a little afraid of Cathal, of someone who could have told such a lie. But then they moved closer to each other, stripped each other's faces and ran their tongues over each other's lips. They would go to see his adoptive parents, of course she would go with him, but first they would find his real mother and then he would feel better.

Regina was surprised when both Cathal and Maolíosa arrived on her doorstep; she had expected only Maolíosa.

When the day came for Cathal to meet his mother, Maolíosa packed the clothes that she thought he should wear. Cathal wanted Maolíosa to be with him, so she dressed in a grey blouse, a pair of black linen trousers, and her good jacket, which she had got from the cleaners just in time before they closed for the weekend. Phew! She talked about lots of emergencies like this in order to distract him, and her. He wore dark green cord trousers, a faintly tinted loose silk shirt and a new jacket that had cost Maolíosa nearly the earth. He looked lovely.

They were meeting on a Saturday. Cathal and his mother would spend half an hour together first, then they would join Maolíosa in the foyer of Buswell's Hotel, they would have a drink, well, they didn't know whether she drank or not, maybe she totally disapproved, stop being nervous, Cathal, it will be all right, maybe she won't like the idea of us living together, well, she can hardly object, Maolíosa tittered, and knew that that was a terrible thing to say but you had to laugh all the same, then they would go for a meal and it will be all right, Cathal, stop fretting.

Afterwards what shocked Maolíosa most was how well they all had handled it. All of them. Maolíosa was sitting, trying to watch the door without looking at it. Cathal came in, he looked only a little nervous. Maolíosa stood up. But the woman with him was Maolíosa's mother. As far as Maolíosa could remember, she and her mother dropped their mouths open together and then put their hands over their eyes in unison, pretending that they were fixing their hair, wishing that they could draw all reality into that space between their eyes and the palms of their hands. That way, it could harm no one. They reached blindly for their seats, her mother less blindly than her. Cathal looked at them for a long minute before he realised. He hit the side of his head with an index finger that had jammed stiff as iron and also reached for a seat. They all had brandy.

'I suspected, only for a minute, that it was you,' Maolíosa's mother said to her. 'Once, when Miss Clarke was talking to me, but I thought it simply couldn't be possible. I suspected again when I met' – she floundered her hand – 'this young man, but by then it was too late. Better to face it now than when you would bring him home to see us.'

She fixed her eyes then on an infinite point behind their heads and made her plea. She didn't ask Cathal, nor Maolíosa for that matter, for forgiveness; Maolíosa thought later, wasn't that strange, wasn't that brave of her really? She spoke in a voice that Maolíosa had never heard before.

'How could I have thought that I could have him for keeps? A man like that could give me the nerve to look through him, right down into his eyes – as if I were above him – past his big heart, hesitating for as long as I could manage without being blinded, and the smooth silk stomach of him and then say, can I hold you, can I really put you inside me? and him to say, oh yes, oh yes, any time, any time. I had known slaps on the face and news of another war, how could I have thought that my time had come? All the while that I was licking across his tongue, ice-cream-eating fashion, and sliding me down so that the tip of him would fill my heart, he must have been looking over my shoulder for others to whom he would give nerve. He liked giving nerve as a gift. So when I found a little of him growing where he had been, my heart was already closed. I couldn't look at a child like him when I would never now have him. How could I? How could I? Don't look at me like that, please. You should understand. Maybe not, maybe not, maybe you've never loved a man like I loved him. Isn't it a strange thing, then, you've never loved this boy like I loved . . . ?

Her voice tapered into the silence.

She refused another brandy, the train was going soon. She left quite steady-footed. Cathal and Maolíosa had one more brandy each and then they walked home together, holding hands, shaking a little at their knees.

Regina Clarke is now paid by the government to find people's mothers.

She should have known when he said, smiling, for the third time during the interview, 'A lot of our boys join the army.'

She did actually. But then she should have known that Ben meant it when he said, 'If you make an ass out of me like that again, out you go on your ear.'

She did actually. At least Smiley Boots here was going to give her the job. She thought Smiley Boots in order to give herself confidence.

'When can you start, Miss Raftery?'

'Ms.'

'Sorry?'

'Ms. Ms Raftery.'

His face dropped into what looked like thunder. The sudden change made his cheekbone tic. I've blown it, she thought, but maybe we could come to some arrangement, I'll ignore his tic if he ignores my unreasonable desire to be addressed like a human being, forgetting for a minute that she wasn't one of the arrangers. Going through the gates she saw a clump of bindweed. Imagine if that jumped up and wrapped itself around her neck, making her gasp for air. Air, stale as it could sometimes be, was better than choking.

So started Rosaleen Raftery on a skimming spree across the minds of the pupils of Rosario's Tech for Boys.

During the first few weeks she got sick in the mornings.

She was frightened by the nest of open mouths in front of her, no names, no idea of what to do if they spat at the blackboard when her back was turned, which they sometimes did, rolled up bits of paper, soaked them and spat them at the blackboard either directly from their mouths or through the barrels of their pens. But within a month she was ready to start each day. She would prove that there could be more for them than their perceived lot. She would like them, even if it killed her. By god, she would like them. She now knew who was who, who couldn't read at all, who couldn't do joined-up writing, who lived in the orphanage down the road, whose father was in jail. She knew that the staff-room verdicts on individual pupils were as much searches for reasons as prejudice. 'Pius O'Brien? He's from a broken home too?' Rosaleen found out that the ones from the smithereened houses were more often than not the very ones who had one room standing for themselves.

The boys would have liked her to be marmy so they could stick pins in her or spit at the blackboard with good reason, but she knew better. She would tighten the rules of love, throw them out, pull them in. She might even make these boys smile at her. They hadn't seen too much of that. This was not a school with happy teachers. No kindness was ever shown in its corridors. Even in the staff room the teachers were afraid. But in her room things were beginning to change. She had made two disparaging remarks about the army. Ben would have been proud of how she had slipped them in. She had mentioned them early in the day. The boys were cold in the mornings. They stood like single blades of grass frozen stiff. If one of their breaths crossed another's,

113

hell and Rosaleen paid. The sneers would have lacerated any delicate hearts if they had not already been calloused. By half past nine the thaw was well set. The toughs had escaped from whatever bit of innocence that sleep had forced on them. Those who were determined to forge a character for themselves had begun to test bits of it out on each other, on her. This testing, herein surely lay the secret.

The sky was pickled with frost one morning. It would have been a decisive day if this had been the country, a no-nonsense, sharp, do-what-you-have-to-do day. The frost bit into Rosaleen's despair, waking her up. Today will be good. I swear today will be good. She hopped over the weed at the gate.

'We will write about an ordinary day in our lives.'

Half a dozen boys grunted, more nipped and punched each other, the usual response to a teacher's first words of the day, the rest ignored her.

'As I said, we will write about an ordinary day'. That's twice she'd said that. 'Me as well. I will start my essay by saying . . .'

A sudden daring silence came out of their mouths and eyes. OK, come on, Miss, say something interesting to us, surprise us, come on, Miss. The next ten seconds would decide which way the silence was to go.

'I will start my essay by saying . . .'

'But Miss, nothing ever happens us.'

David and Leo remembered exactly together, like synchronised swimmers, some unsolved insult – hey you, just you wait, pigface. The two boys searched frantically for the words they hated most, splittering insults that would

114

have to do until they could find the worst possible one.

'... by saying, Last night I rang my boyfriend, my ex-boyfriend, again. I knew that he was out because I had just seen him walk through my cul-de-sac – it's only a cul-de-sac for cars. I rang to hear his voice on the answering machine. He still had my name on the tape...'

Complete silence.

'Now. There is a blank page. At this minute you could be anyone, you are no one, or at least we don't see you. It is up to you to build yourselves on to these pages. Paint your own pictures of yourselves.'

They started to mutter, but it was a slightly confused mutter and lacked the foundation necessary to turn a mutter into a roar. Had she really said that? they wondered. Before they'd finished mumbling, she had placed a blank page on each desk. Using a separate page rather than their copybooks invested the exercise with importance.

'As I was saying, his voice hadn't changed at all.'

'How long since you'd heard it, Miss?'

'Three months, Liam. Now. You can start your ordinary day by talking about sounds of voices in the morning. Who speaks first, what that person says, who likes to be quiet in the morning ... a likely tale ...'

'But Miss, we told you, nothing happens us.'

'Well, nothing happened to me last night except ...'

'Ah, go on, Miss, tell us.'

'Except I watched television, corrected your essays and ...'

'And what, Miss?'

She could feel a leer gathering steam.

'We will see when all your essays are done.' She looked at them straight out from under her eyes. What could they do? She had won this time. They would write now, not because it was of any use to them, what use are stupid essays? but because they wanted to find out what she had the nerve to write. She had read their minds well. It was a great week. She made them write and rewrite and they did so gladly because they began to believe her, that this was them. They handed her pieces each day, some pinched, some upturned, some already hardened into stone.

But then David Lean's father wrote his own piece and it landed into their classroom like a nasty missile from outside, dragging them back to the meagreness of the acceptable. 'Dear Miss, I'll not have you getting my son to write out everything we're doing here. I know what's going on, trying to nose your way into our house. You do your job during school and I'll do mine after in my own house.' He also sent a copy to the headmaster. She couldn't hide it from the boys either, because David, not knowing what else to do, had already swelled out telling them in the school yard before the bell went. Me da wrote to the headmaster.

The boys, although they weren't sure why, went with David and his father, because how could they not? Against her, the teacher. They mumbled all that day in class. They would not write. On the way out Mark Turner said, 'And you never showed us the last of yours, Miss.'

'Good on ya, Twansey,' a back voice that was now pushing the others said.

'Stop pushing, fatface.'

'I was going to,' she said, and meant it.

The headmaster said that the army was not the sort of place where men spent their time thinking about ordinary days. He tried to say it with a measure of lightheartedness, the softest Rosaleen had ever seen him, but she snorted. After she was outside the gate.

And so the class went back to its original battlefield. Rosaleen stole minutes to catch her breath, when the boys momentarily forgot to fight themselves or her. Watching their bent heads, she could imagine innocent things living there. Seven fours, Miss? Twenty-eight. She had always seen numbers standing in rows, beginning east to west, one to twenty. Twenty to thirty, west to east, thirty to forty east to west. So when she would get to age twenty the hardest part would be over. Did any of them see numbers like this?

Why was there no one to take a picture of her standing here in front of her adversaries? They were quiet now. How unbelievably quiet! How many seconds would it last? Should she be thinking of something to do when they would inevitably lift their heads, something to stop them from tearing this room apart? Like them? She was afraid of them mostly. People had less important pictures taken, ones at the boat in Dún Laoghaire that could be anywhere, ones at parties that were forgotten before the film was developed, holding-hands ones that would mock them from the bottom of the pile unless they were unsuperstitious enough to burn them. Why not a picture of her here? No one ever saw this, a teacher, only one teacher, five feet three, against twenty-five boys, one hundred and thirty-one feet six.

There was a photograph of her and Ben on the kitchen wall. They looked well, with his head on her shoulder. But

117

that wasn't true, she had pulled his head down a minute before the flash went, just so they could have one picture where they looked as if they really liked each other. One picture wasn't too much to set up, and the smile on his face was really from surprise at what she'd just done.

Why couldn't they let her daydream, even for a few minutes? How could they fight her even on that? Daydreaming was important. They could drop out any time to daydream. If she noticed, she certainly never drew their attention back. They might learn more in that faraway place, and even if they did not, it kept them quiet. But her, oh no, they'd never let her daydream. She drew her eyes back and they looked at her silently. They had been looking at her for how long? Oh the dears, the little lovely dears, they had been camera enough.

'Thank you, boys.'

'It's all right, Miss, any time.'

They laughed together.

But the next morning something ugly had planted itself in the room. She could smell it when she came in. She could never be sure what it was, or how bad it was going to be, only that it was there. The air crackled. That meant the intercom. They stopped slicing each other and gave one minute's attention. The headmaster's voice was clear, uncivilian.

'You will all have heard of the fire in the disco last night. Three of our past pupils were killed. Four of our past pupils were injured. There are brothers and sisters of our present pupils among the dead and injured. You will all attend mass at lunchtime.'

The intercom switched off. He hadn't said their names.

There was a brief silence and then words spoken in hushed bitter voices. And this new inconsiderateness, mixed in with whatever they had been feeling before the interruption, sent boys hurling at each other. Why should they care? If he had come around to each classroom and spoken their names, it would have been different. Let them murder each other, Rosaleen said to herself. She couldn't possibly come between them anyway. Was it for this that she had put in years of learning how to learn and then learning how to teach, that she had in the beginning suffered humiliations which came up in welts on her body when she slept? The fight controlled itself because of what had happened last night in a disco, a place that had the same attitude to them as had this school. Mass was a relief.

A week later normal hostilities had resumed. There was one immune boy, Patrick. He had sprouted ideas early and now he was in love. With a girl called Nessa. He was having his first summer although it was February. Why had this never happened before? Why Nessa? What was it? He had built for himself a private dream around his desk. It had a town in it, songs, people to pass on his way up the road where he would see her. He tried to concentrate on history. It was his favourite subject. Rosaleen would not have believed that there could be such a thing as a favourite subject in this classroom. But as soon as a key word fell, there were thousands of them, he would lose the grip of solid daily things and find himself being cajoled up the street again.

Rosaleen wanted to be able to go home to Ben. It used to be that she could go home to him and talk about the ozone layer, or some such disaster, or poor Salman Rushdie, or the plight of Muslim women, we'd better not forget them, and also the fact that, let's not forget this, our fingers aren't clean either, and he'd put his arms around her and say nothing is going to happen, you're just a worrier, and she'd believe him that nothing terrible was going to happen. He was right too.

Sometimes Rosaleen was too tired to care what happened. She would stand here and let them kill themselves if they wanted to. The noise whispered below the surface, the boys sniffed a lot, the noise gathered speed like a barrel running down a hill. She looked out the window past their faces, which she found just too raw today. She fixed her eyes on the only piece of grass to be seen from these windows, in fact, from the entire school. No matter how you craned your neck, from no matter which place, you couldn't see grass. It was so small, so far away, she was never quite sure if it was grass. What if it was someone's roof and they painted it red some weekend? She narrowed her eyes and pushed her way over the miles, forcing herself to see flowers coming up on what might be a green roof. The noise began to thump, it was going to crack. She said, to the square of grass, in a low oily voice: 'Gentlemen, will you please be quiet.' She could have slipped on the words. 'Gentlemen', and the word created its own noise. Not one of them dared resist it. And it became apparent that she meant it, because she continued to look at the grass. Some of them looked out the window, following her eyes, but they could see nothing. They fiddled, giggled, only a little, passed notes to each other, drew pictures, shocked that this could be asked of them. When the bell went they said, 'Miss, can we go now?' although they didn't want to. 'Yes,' she said.

And in the morning she believed in them. Could this be the same class? She could see into them, they were full of hearts, veins, livers, they had toes, foreheads and elbows, they liked her, they wanted her to teach them things, they thought those things important. Those things were important. Geography. But they weren't too interested where Balbriggan or Maynooth were, she could tell. She said, 'I'll not have you making asses of yourselves with girls from all over the country' – they'd never thought of girls being from all over the country before – 'I'll not have you saying, "You're from Tralee? Really? We went on holidays there to Roscommon once."' So she cleared the desks to the outer edge of the room and stood them in lines and gave them hands to point to where the places were and she gave them girls to match the places. Sally Shovelin from Sligo, Bettina Toal from Tyrone, Kitsy Kinnane from Kerry. Then she sat them down and they drew themselves on maps in Rosario's Tech for Boys, and they filled in their girls' names and places and what those girls' lives were like in those particular places.

'May I ask, Miss Raftery, what your class was doing standing in line all over the room when they should have been sitting?'

'Practising for the army.'

Five minutes late and the rain was lashing down. Six minutes late. Now, if he finds this out, he'll have one up his sleeve for months. What's that line outside the door? As Rosaleen got closer, and closer, she could pick out boys, her boys. Their clothes – skimpy, too thin, too-small jackets, or just jumpers – were soaked into them. Their hair streaked with wet. The hungrier ones were shivering.

'What's the meaning of this?'

'Well, Miss, you didn't turn up on time. Look what's happened to us.' The tears in their voices were of cold as much as of rage.

'Miss Raftery, in future, classes will stay outside in the morning until their teacher arrives. So it will be in the interest of the teacher to come on time.'

'What if they get soaking wet?'

'I got the idea yesterday when I saw your class standing in such neat rows.'

For the rest of the day Rosaleen stood with her head at the square window in the door. She wanted to keep her nose pressed to it. She wanted to stick her tongue out at him every time he passed.

'Miss Raftery, I wouldn't worry too much about it,' he would say to her face, 'it's good training.'

'Like the army, I suppose?'

'You seem to have an inordinate dislike of the army. Why would that be? They do at least get trained.'

'Trained my eye! Driving around the country, after money, cooped up in vans or lying in ditches along the border with black shoe polish on their faces.'

Rosaleen wrote on the blackboard:

PRISONS, CRIME AND PUNISHMENT
WHY NOT TO GET INTO TROUBLE

'You mean, why not to get caught, Miss!'

'You can discuss that among yourselves. I'm not your moral guardian. I just want to tell you why not to get into trouble. And while we are at this we should be able to squeeze in a bit of history.'

PRISONS, SOUTH TO NORTH

CORK

LIMERICK

PORTLAOISE

MOUNTJOY

ARBOUR HILL

LOUGHAN HOUSE

ARMAGH (now MAGHABERRY)

LONG KESH

CRUMLIN ROAD

MAGILLIGAN CAMP

'And once there was a ship too,' she finished, moving to the back of the class. They all looked at the list.

'It's an awful lot of prisons, Miss.'

She was still standing at the back of the room when the headmaster walked in, so she couldn't get to the blackboard to wipe off the evidence.

His eyes took in that she hadn't left out the contentious ones. He called her to the door.

'Interesting display on your blackboard, Miss Raftery.'

'I thought they'd need to know where they are, for when they join the army, sir.'

'Excuse me for interrupting,' he said to the boys as he beckoned her outside. 'And may I ask what made you think you could take Education for Living classes? We have people trained for that.'

'Trained to say nothing.'

Rosaleen felt her contract sparkling into thin air.

'Miss Raftery, take your books home with you. And could you clear your locker out thoroughly. We are going to paint it at the weekend, and we don't want any of your things hanging around.'

'Only my locker?' Rosaleen asked, smiling.

'Only yours.'

GIVEN TIME

Nuala stood there for a while, staring at him, then went downstairs, cooked breakfast and brought it back to bed. The breakfast was lovely, grilled rashers, tomatoes, mushrooms done properly, the view from the bed was fine. Who could this have happened to but Nuala? Who? Oh, I suppose it could have happened to anyone. But who could face it? Nuala will. Given time, Nuala will.

*   *   *

Nuala McCooey's husband had left her on a February day. For five years afterwards she considered it a bad month. It made her feel as if there was an apple stuck in her throat. From the first to the twenty-eighth she wondered what sort of conversation he was having with his new girlfriend. Was she saying, 'February makes me nervous, that's the month you left your wife'? Was he, the faithless blaggard, answering, 'Now, you don't think that it was because of the time of the year that I left her?' and was he then smiling at her and was she giggling back? On the first of March things always looked up. She was well rid of him. During that five years there was one leap year and it seemed cruel in a ludicrous way.

The weekend that Fergal brought her to meet his parents and sisters they teased him about snoring. She blushed, she thought it interesting, just another interesting thing about him – God, when would it end? She'd never heard anyone really snore. They also teased him about being mean, about being selfish. They trotted out his failings in a good-humoured way, aired them in front of her, shook them a bit to make noise so she might hear them, but they need not have bothered, because her ears as well as her eyes were glazed over with love. They married, and liked each other well for a year or two or more, then they started bumping into one another in bed and side-stepping during the day. But they were all right. They read books, naturally – they were both well educated and their jobs (teachers in a col-lege, a third-level institution that wasn't quite a university yet) demanded it.

They read nearly all the same books, although she never read about photography and he never read poetry. 'No time for it,' he said – and he didn't mean, not enough time. She said that photography was the consolation of the thin-skinned – they had to have proof of experience. Nothing went down too deep in them, so they couldn't remember well.

He thought she had become sarky. One evening she threw a book of short stories down. 'Another one at it, visiting his ex-wife. We don't do that sort of thing here. If you were lucky enough to have an ex-husband, you wouldn't go visit-ing him.' And then she washed the dishes quite happily, blowing suds from the top of the wine glass and humming to herself. She didn't like him to wash the dishes any more, she saved them up for herself against the boredom. Maybe that evening marked the beginning of the end. They stopped doing things together, most noticeably, going to the pictures. She felt that the fantasy land of the cinema raised expectations and the let-down afterwards was too much to bear.

After ten years they burned out – not bad, some people burn out after ten days. There are a lot of ashes after ten years. They finally bored themselves and each other to ignition point with small talk, not that the talk itself, because it was small, was of any less value than most talk, just that they were bored anyway and couldn't get enthusiastic about boiling an egg in the morning. It was only a matter of who would do it first. Fergal did. Nuala and her friend Betty discussed the student who was making the most embarrassing sidles-up to him. Every time he passed she fixed her eyes on his back as if through looking she would be able to soak up bits of him and swallow them.

'Would you mind if he did?' Betty asked.

'They're welcome to each other,' Nuala humphed, in the way that people can before the fact.

Fergal began to read articles and stories about people having affairs, he read *Bornholm Night Ferry*, he indulged in films that claimed to have insight into passion. He spent a night with the student who lived around the corner from himself and Nuala. He liked the layout of the house, exactly the same as his own, and joked to the student that he would be able to walk blindfolded to her bed and know he was in the right room. She didn't bat an eyelid. If this thing worked out, who knows, it might save his marriage. But the place was too small for that. If you had sex with your husband, the town would know it in the morning. So

Fergal was found out.

It took Nuala five years to recover, not the full five years in time, but spread from the beginning to the end of five years, with particular dreary listlessness and unexpected sobs rising up in her during the Februarys. Five years was reasonable really, half a year for each one with him. After that, she envied no one his company, his arms, his comfort, his penis, to be brutally honest. She finally even felt sorry for the student who had apparently collapsed into a pale trance when Fergal decided, after six months, that enough was enough. Nuala eventually fell in love again with a man who fell in love with her, perhaps to prove that she still believed in something. Before that, Fergal moved to teach in Aberdeen university, for a year at least, he said, having come off the saddest in the end. Aberdeen could hardly be called the centre of the universe, which is where he thought he was going the first night he slept with the student. Nuala stayed in the house.

How did she fall in love again and what did it mean? But first, the five years.

Nuala spent that February, and March, and April, blubbering inconsolably, telling and retelling, mixing up day and night, drinking brandy, losing weight and putting her friendship with Betty through a fine-comb test. But she woke up one morning, heard, as if for the first time, a bird singing, forgot to remind herself that she wasn't thinking about Fergal and scrubbed herself in the bath. A shiny new month was dawning. She had things to forget, to rub out of her life as if they'd never been, dreams to undream, which is the hardest. That can give a person rheumatism. At times she could clearly see herself unravelling herself. This shocked her. But in other ways it was good, because she had, among other things, seen far too many sad happenings happen.

Nuala started to go on dates, that's what she called them, the word was right for the passing of time. As soon as she stopped calling the men by the wrong names she knew she was getting somewhere. A man named Eoin told her in the morning that he'd never imagined women liking sex so much. Her eyebrows shot up under her fringe – well, it was new breakfast conversation anyway. He was intent on chat, she would have preferred to rush the pleasantries and close the door on last night. Then there was Declan, who kissed as if to warm his freezing lips, and Neal, who unashamedly saw the meal or the pictures or the drink as the Dale Carnegie handshake – remember her name, agree with her, get on with it. And then there were some terrible names. One morning she discovered that the man was called Ernie. Surely she couldn't have heard that last night.

She found out that it was easier than you'd think and harder than you'd think to get men to bed. Whatever the difficulties, she got them, although she could never quite believe this, and often they were gone before she realised that they had been there.

She was on a scattered road to recovery. It might look dismal to those in love or those not needing love. It might bring derogatory remarks within inches of her back from the shocked. Mad jealous was her reply. Once, in the staff room, in the middle of a desultory conversation about computers, a teacher said, 'This is Ireland, you know – not

California', then looked surprised at herself. It was as if the words had been pushed into her mouth by someone else and she had to get them out no matter what. Everyone looked at Nuala. Mad jealous, she thought. That night she sat naked on Fergal's high stool – he'd bought it after a knee injury, it was easier to sit not bending his knee – she was being touched by and was touching Neal . . . Na na, na na na. Nuala was getting a past.

Her sister came home on holidays from Brussels. She didn't do things like Nuala did, ah no, she wore skirts that met expectations, that overlapped in the middle. Nuala had forgotten what she herself generally wore. Of course, she knew what clothes were in the wardrobe, but she couldn't remember buying them or not having them. She forgot other things too; she forgot to cut her toenails until the one beside the big one cut the smaller one beside it; she forgot to go to the hairdresser's (but that could have been because she first overheard about Fergal in the hairdresser's); she forgot who wrote ode on 'Intimations of Immortality'; she forgot she was at her mother's and went into long loud stretches as if she was Jesus in *The Life of Brian.* Her sister and her sister's skirts unnerved her. Her sister wanted her to remember how to behave.

Nuala tippled purposefully towards oblivion and went to bed with the wrong man again. She had a sordid little night that triumphed over nothing but time. When he left she said, 'Well, that was inappropriate.' That's how good I've got at this, she thought, I can say 'inappropriate' as if all I had just done was give a wrong answer. She went walking by the sea at Sandymount but saw nothing except dogs shitting and people getting old, until a wind came up and started playing with the water. She watched it scoot across the waves, turning the water's colour as it chased over it, the way neon lights career open-mouthed around signs, gobbling up any darkness, anything that is not flashy. She stared at it, this dancing wind that changed the sea's face, and was overcome by the thought of a long, lovely sleep. Perhaps she should have a rest.

While she was doing all these things to help her forget Fergal, a life was being lived, passed, gone through. Hers. Days, weeks, were being gobbled up. She went home and thought, that was a recovered day. What's a recovered day – a day reclaimed or a day just lived? Nuala got her hand-bag ready for morning, tidied it, threw out the rubbish. It must be a terrible thing to go around the world without a handbag. She changed the sheets and went to bed.

One day, between classes, Nuala tried to count the number of men she'd slept with since Fergal left. She took a pen and started to write their first names down – M, J, E, C, D, G, B, J, E, K, N . . . She felt seasick. What excuse would she have if someone looked over her shoulder? Names for children – my sister's pregnant, or a crossword? a list of my uncles? When she went home she looked through her diaries. Yes, she appeared to have lived a com-paratively normal life, no one would guess, there was the occasional unplaceable telephone number but, other than that nothing strange. It was interesting, the what that was not in her diaries.

She started taking notes on promiscuity, set up headings. How Do Certain Types Of Alcohol Affect It? Promiscuity

And The Weather; How Widespread Is It? Promiscuity And The Cycle; Promiscuity And Secrecy; Is It Bad For You? Is It Good For You? And subnotes on other things learned, Men And Contraception; Lines That Herald Impotence; Good Sex; Men And Their Mothers; Men And Me; Why Men? Good Sex. She stuck the headings up on the walls of her kitchen, just for an hour, looked at them and wondered what a person could make of them. She grabbed them down quickly when the doorbell rang.

Later that year a thin slice of light appeared in the shape of Donal, all smiles, all love, all chat, all hands. He wanted to understand something. He asked questions continuously about Nuala and Fergal, none about that recent past she had collected for herself.

'But why, really?'

'The last row, the weariness of it. Most rows are the same as the ones that went before, but so is the last straw. Fergal said that a successful relationship between a man and a woman happens over years when they've learned what to do about her non-stop need for talk (that was mine), her need for change and for things to remain the same all at the one time versus his for silence at home and a quick screw.'

'I don't think you talk too much,' Donal said.

'All we ever changed was the position of this bed,' Nuala said.

Donal rubbed her stomach and looked at the ceiling.

'Fergal asked me would I forgive him. I said, what does forgive mean? I told him to look in the mirror on the way out and say sorry.'

Nuala fell in love with Donal.

'What does love mean?' she asked him. He said he didn't know.

They lived more or less happily ever after for three years. Nothing serious went wrong between them. Their hands still felt good sitting inside each other – it was the smoother parts of their skin touching that made them jump back. He didn't mention forgiveness when he was moving out, nor did she. There was no need. They are still the best of friends.

Nuala's face began growing into that interesting look of one whose love has been with end, twice.

The status of the third-level college changed to university. Nuala got a rise and moved house. She chose the house carefully. Betty helped her. They loved doing it. Nuala liked shaking her head and saying, no, that wouldn't do, as if she had always made important choices. She signed the contracts with a sure hand, and put the key into the front door with the same certain fingers. She walked around her home, happy with it and the sometimes awkward resolutions of her life that she'd managed to come through. She looked forward to her new job, less sixteenth-century Tudor lyric, more Latin American fiction.

It was last Saturday before she could lie in bed late, pull back the heavy drapes and look out unobserved through the net curtains at her back garden. There were abandoned drills where vegetables had grown. Maybe she would? There were foxgloves, a healthy virginia creeper, clumps of unknown bushes, some mallow, a sturdy pyracantha. There was a rhubarb patch and a growing apple tree. There was space and light and more light. Oh, it was going to be great. It was that kind of day when Nuala felt her life could be parcelled up, the ends of it tidied, packaged neatly as you would a gift, a bow could be put on it, it could sit satisfied, pleased and waiting to please. Leaning over the edge had done her no harm.

The next-door neighbour was on his knees weeding, his head bent to the ground. It was a familiar, homely sort of head, it would be nice having new homely neighbours. He stood up and turned around to go into his shed. Nuala put her hands flat on her face, as if by doing that she could somehow push back into nothing what she had just seen. He, her new neighbour, was Fergal. She stood there and watched him, then tiptoed back to the middle of the room. I don't believe it, I do not believe it. He was Fergal.

THE LAST CONFESSION

I swear to you, she was absolutely normal. Is absolutely normal. If I tell you a little about our childhood and how normal we were, and if I don't tell you until later what she actually did, you'll say that I cheated you into thinking that she was normal, but then, if I tell you first, you'll think of her as the person who did what she did and you won't take in just how normal she was. Is. I argue this out with myself a lot, will I think about her today as she was or is that fooling myself? or will I think about the mess she has created for me, all of us, herself? but then that is denying the fact, the truth, that she is a perfectly normal woman.

My sister. I am three years older than her, there are the two of us. I was adored because I was the boy, she because she was the girl. We adored each other, maybe I adored her a little more than she did me because she took streaks of the sun with her into rooms even in wintertime. We talked lots, we liked to tease each other. That's an odd way of looking at it, we loved to tell each other, although we only said that so the other person would say it back. We loved the idea that we might be odd. There wasn't a hope in hell. Sometimes when she did things that I had just done I wanted to say copycat because I felt that I had nothing of my own – my mother when telling stories to the neighbours would even mix up which of us had said what – but I didn't dare because I was afraid to really hurt her and anyway, there were advantages – if what I was doing and saying was worth copying, then I was making my presence felt, wasn't I?

Other times, when I would suggest doing something daring, like jumping from the top of the hay on to the barn floor, she would say, yes, you've talked me into it, although I wouldn't have tried persuasion at all. She sometimes used sentences like that, just to see how her saying them sounded, they were such un-Irish sentences, sentences that were being thrown about in movies, but we had no movies in Monaghan. Where she could have learned them I don't know. She was much quicker than me at things like that, picking up words, ideas. Particularly when the sun shone. Later she told me this was because she's Aquarian but I let that pass. I felt it was just the light. A day when the road was dry, it was even white, the sun lit the whole way down it, burned would be too strong a word, you could imagine that there was dust in the air it was so hot, although this would have been a gross exaggeration. Our shadows were there in front of us – remnants of the dark winter just gone – we danced on top of each other's until we got irritated because we could never dance on our own. Or get rid of it. We made them walk up hedges. Actually this shadow-dancing served more than one purpose. If we were really annoyed, we could screw our heels viciously into each other's heads, and pretend it was a joke. One time she merged our shadows into one. She made me promise never to fall out with her. It wasn't hard to make me do that, I had no intentions of it.

For a while, when she was thirteen and I was sixteen, our

friendship changed. She still loved me but I spent my time trying to impress her, which is not love. I thought it was, but now know better. After a time, I gave that nonsense up and went back to being her real friend. She seemed to have learned a lot, she talked even more than before. I couldn't keep up with her – even normally I cannot talk and think at the same time. I have to think it out first and then I forget it when it comes to talking if I'm not given a long time to say it slowly. I bite the inside of my mouth with agitation at times like this. But she could talk and think and also draw my attention to the fact that the inside of my mouth would end up in ridges if I didn't stop that, which only made me worse.

But with all this talking she could still figure things out – as I said, she could talk and think together. She always made me feel as if I was following her, when I know that wasn't really true. But I had to hand it to her, when I grew my hair half an inch below my collar she fought for me day and night. She fought so long and hard with our parents that you'd think she was the one who had offended the rules. (Rules is too mild a word, so, too, is way of life.) And yet, even when she was fighting with them, for herself now, too, about the length of her skirts, she could defend them to me. I said, out of their hearing, of course, that if they both stopped smoking there'd be more money for clothes for us and wasn't it their duty? She said no, that parents also had rights of their own and they were entitled to their cigarettes if they wanted to kill themselves. On the subject of which she never liked to linger. Part of the work of maturing involved forcing yourself to be interested in who that was who died yesterday, who they were related to, what age they were and what killed them. But she would have none of this, she said that there was more to life than dying and she had better things to be thinking about. She said once that she loathed the way people said 'Do you know what I think is very sad?' with delight and glee in their voices. Really loathed it. I remember the day she said that. I should have believed myself and known that that day was as monumental as I thought it was, us standing there with one foot each against the wall, discussing death, life and love. I should have believed myself. I could have enjoyed it, too, because life was not so complicated then.

I went to a new city – I should say, I went to a city. I still sometimes remember the pride of daily arriving in the right street, the attention I gave to details that I cannot now see (I cannot even recall what the details were), the feeling that my life was one long undeserved festival. But I missed some things, my sister mostly. She passed through my flat on her way to her new city. We talked nearly all night. She asked me did I ever hear the way when one person says to another, 'I can't stand such and such' or 'I hate when . . .' or 'I wouldn't have that . . .' and the other person says, 'I'm the same.' She said she always felt like saying, well, I'm not. We also talked about losing our faith, everyone talked about that at the time, and how wonderful it was to be rid of all that hypocrisy. It was a lovely night and I saw her off the next morning, excited for her, she was so delighted.

She spent five years away. I lived an ordinary life and, I suppose, missing her sharpness, I slipped and let it become more ordinary than it had to be. By the time she came home

I had become certain that I knew everything I needed to know. I was solid. And I think we had lost our unconditional love. We talked to, not with, each other. But we still loved each other. Maybe I was a little afraid of her because she had stayed faithful to the overwhelming wonder that we had had when we were young. I couldn't stand the incessantness of that wonder. She would sit down, ready to talk for hours about something political, not just ready, compelled, it was our duty, our lives. I felt that it was one big fairly empty game, someone else's, things were and would be. She looked at me sadly but took it in her stride and then started talking about our personal lives, she could still do that too. My unconditional love came back.

When I told her that I was getting married, she said that personally she found marriage obscene. It was built on men owning women, I said it worked both ways, she said like hell it does and you know it. She narrowed her eyes and lips closer together than I'd ever seen them before when she said that. I knew, if I was truthful to myself, that she had a point but I wanted a private place in which to have my worries, a place where I could break down without being seen or remarked upon.

She came to the wedding and was the most gracious sister-in-law I have ever seen, wishing my now wife every good that she could imagine, fearful for her, even though it was me that was the husband! I was very torn, for a second, when it came to getting into the going-away car, knowing that she somehow felt disappointed in me, but you can imagine which side I took – it's not every day you get married. As my wife and I pulled away (embarrassed by such ancient innuendo and really us nearly tired looking at each other naked), she put on a superior look but I knew that she didn't mean it, it was just defence against isolation.

Ah yes, it had been a long five years, the longest.

About a year after that, I got the strangest request. I was asked to come to the Bishop's Palace in Drumcondra, on the Drumcondra Road, nearly opposite where the Lemon's Sweet Factory was, still is, but nobody works in it now, so I suppose you wouldn't really call it a factory. There was an embossed shield on the notepaper, although the envelope was plain. I jokingly said to my wife, you haven't filed for an annulment have you? I was at a loss to know what on earth it could be about, but they very politely wouldn't tell me over the phone, yet they nearly begged me to turn up. There was no fear that I wouldn't, because my curiosity was well and truly whetted.

When I reached the gate I started getting nervous, it was like being called to account for all your movements, your sins, before you had died. I have always believed that I will be able to manage a reasonable number of excuses – that is, if there's a God, you understand – on the actual day itself, death will have given me a new maturity, but to have to do it before dying, I wasn't prepared for that. I had never been at the gates before – well, it's not the sort of place that you can be at. It's just there, a looming gate that somehow swallows you.

Actually I tell a lie, I had been there once. I had arranged to meet my sister for a drink on a February night that had been night all day. She rang me at work and said, very fast, that she would be at a picket outside the Bishop's Palace and could I pick her up there. See you. So I had to go. When I arrived more snow had fallen, it vainly tried to look white. It was so cold I could have cried. But the women were cheerful, they were up against such odds they laughed a lot. More than me, I had to admit, who was happier. I presumed. She was like a ball of ice when she got into the car, but a few hot whiskeys and she said she was thawed out. I wasn't, but I let it go. Then I said, would you like another drink somewhere nicer? and she said delightedly, yes, as long as it's in Dún Laoghaire, at the North Wall docks or the airport.

Well, I was further than the gate this time. The avenue is, quite simply, frightening. I mustn't be the first person to think this, because after Vatican Two, they cut down trees leading up to lots of chapel gates so that people would feel more part of the whole thing. Less frightened. When I think about that day, I dwell on my reactions to the avenue because they were the most and the least important.

The bishop said that there was a problem with my sister and could I tell him something about her. I said tersely, I beg your pardon, meaning, who the *hell* do you think you are and *what* in God's name do you take me for? He then said, we thought it would be best to speak to you rather than your parents. I said, *sorry?* meaning, are you threatening me? (In the circumstances this was a bit premature of me.) He said, to get to the point quickly, your sister is threatening us. She has forged some photographs of a few individual priests, in compromising positions; she says she is going to release them to the newspapers. We cannot, of course, allow that. And will not, he added. Perhaps you can help us. I realise this must come as a shock to you, I'm sure

141

you didn't know the character of your sister – I feebly thought, who does this geezer think he is? – so I will leave it with you until tomorrow. But I don't know where she is, I thought, already following orders. I was being dismissed.

When I got outside the door I had a splitting headache. If I could have got my hands on her throat! But then I smiled, just briefly. One evening we had exchanged notions of uncomfortable moments.

'You know, when you hop into the front of a taxi by mistake and the minute you're in there you realise you've done the wrong thing and you want to say to the driver, sorry, I thought it was my own car, but you say nothing and he says nothing and you stare out the window and wish to God the journey was over. You even contemplate climbing into the back seat but that would make it worse. I hate that.'

'Last week I was at this traditional music singing session, proper traditional, and the man beside me started to sing "The Wild Rover" and everyone turned to glare and I wanted to jump up and say, he's not with me, honestly, I swear he's not.'

'Or the doctor intimates to you to take off your clothes and get on the couch, you strip naked, he turns around and says, I only meant your skirt, you blush to a temperature of one hundred and four degrees and he says, but it's all right if you're happy. God, you feel like a flasher of the lowest order, taking advantage of a doctor.'

'Worse than that, I was beside a bank robber one day. Every time I go into the bank now I want to say, look, see me, I'm not a bank robber, I was only beside him.'

Bad moments. Well, this one beats them all.

I sweated for a week, day and night, and had the most terrible dreams day and night. The bishop was in constant contact. It put a strain on my marriage. My wife said that it was one thing being a catholic but quite another having the bishop ring you up every day, it put her off the normal business of living, she said. It certainly changed the atmosphere in our bedroom. Then my sister rang, as they had guessed she would, oh, they always know.

She told me that she'd had a great laugh today because this old man beside her on the bus had blessed himself half way up the Rathmines Road. So she was in Dublin, well, I knew that anyway from the money dropping in. She told him she thought it was a good idea. He said, chuffed, 'Blessing yourself passing the chapel? Yes.' She said, 'Oh I didn't know it was the church, I thought you were blessing yourself passing the Battered Women's Centre.' Shut up, I screamed at her, what the hell do you think you're at? God, how I wished for simplicity just at that minute. I didn't want to know why she had done it. I didn't want to have to make any connections, I just wanted to know what to do next, and I was glad that she was all right.

She said, do you remember the party where we all discussed our last confessions? Yes I remembered. I had waited at the edge of their talk, a sound that was growing in excitement every minute – I must admit some of them were funny – Please Father, I broke the fifth commandment, she had meant to say that she had committed adultery. Afterwards she thought how could he be so calm when he thought she'd killed somebody and she just knew that he

143

wouldn't have taken it so easily if she had got her commandment right. It set her to thinking. Then another voice said, I said, Please Father, I've been heavy petting – what by the way *does* heavy petting mean? – he asked me was I going to marry the man and I nearly jumped out of my skin. Well, give him up then. It was easier to give up the confessions. And the usual tales of the probing priest, and what do you mean by that? and what does he do? and do you take pleasure out of it? I waited so I could tell mine. It was a good one. They all laughed. But I left them. I had only wanted to say it, not get involved. They were taking it too seriously. They seemed to be making out of the conversation a collective harm done to them. And maybe it was, because, after all, my humiliation was not as thorough, the priest was a man. Yes I remembered. Well, I got the idea then, she said. She would take revenge.

And so she tricked three priests, four actually – how many? I moaned – maybe half a dozen. It was easy. She photographed them afterwards when they were asleep, pulled the sheets back and photographed them. She described some of them, their confessions to her, the photos, asking someone to take a photograph of her and one of them without him seeing. Wasn't that dicey? But by then she was as high as a kite on what she was going to do. She said she was doing it to blow apart the *total* hypocrisy – I mean TOTAL – and I got impatient thinking, yes, yes, yes, but you can't do that. I then said, but didn't it bother you, sleeping with priests? yuk; she said that it wasn't only men who could enjoy revenge.

She wouldn't see me; oh please, just so I can talk some

sense into you, no, no, she wouldn't. So they were wrong about that, they said that she would definitely see me.

The following Saturday's papers carried a note to the effect that the photographs existed, an unsigned statement from my sister saying she had no objections to priests having sexual relationships as long as they didn't pretend that they weren't and as long as they admitted it openly and changed the laws accordingly and were as generous to everybody else and stopped fooling the people, etc., etc. The bishops also had a statement about a blackmail note from some nut-case who had constructed a number of photographs she alleged were of priests. They didn't know who she was and preferred to let the matter rest. Didn't know who she was, hah!

Well, how come next morning there were police cars everywhere around our street? They stayed there for a month, so soon the neighbours had the whole story. The gardaí told them, in order to relieve their boredom and to get them on their side. It was unbearable. So we sold our house and moved out here to the wilderness. The neighbours don't see the police cars, there are no neighbours.

My wife doesn't talk about my sister. Neither do I, but oh, I do love to think about her often, sometimes, like now.

PETTY CRIME

All children should have a letter from their father to their mother that they can find some day when they're rooting through boxes looking for something else. This is Brendan Gaffney's children's letter. That is, if their mother doesn't tear it up or burn it. He felt a little seedy writing it, sitting there in the waiting room of the North Wall, watching out from under his eyebrows for the opening of the doors of the Liverpool boat. Seedy, because he knew that he was writing it not just for Mags and the children but also because it made him look innocent. No man running away would be sitting writing a letter. He'd be more likely to be talking to someone, a stranger even, so that he wouldn't look conspicuous, or reading a paper. The *Irish Times*. Criminals don't read the *Irish Times*, not small-time ones anyway. Seedy and something else as well, a man with the bottom knocked out of him, but that's so big to think about, it couldn't be thought about. He looked at his shoes, they were as clean as anything.

Dear Mags,
By the time you get this I'll be safely in Liverpool or somewhere. I'll let you know as soon as I get an address. I know this will upset you but there was nothing else I could have done . . .

Brendan had not always been destined to be skulking

away in the early night. Sixteen years ago he and Margaret Daly married; they went to Las Palmas for their honeymoon and didn't really like it. The first week was OK but the second dragged a bit. If it hadn't been for a couple from Kerry, also on their honeymoons, they would have gone mad.

Part of the reason that the week dragged was because they were dying to get home, home to this great new house which the firm Brendan worked for had almost finished. Because the house was for Brendan, the lads had done all sorts of little extra things, things they had hauled up from the bottoms of their imaginations, brass fittings on the doors, a serving hatch between the kitchen and the dining room, 'For when there's hundreds of little Gaffneys, Brendan, hundreds . . .' And the bedroom! You could sleep in the wardrobe and still there was space for a dressing table, a bedside locker, which the lads had bought for them, guffawing for days afterwards, and the bed. Their bed, where they could stay on a Sunday morning; indeed, they could stay in it all day Sunday as long as they pulled the curtains open at some reasonable hour. Mags's mother had said that there was great liberty in the house, he liked Mags's mother.

In the beginning the years had gone in so satisfactorily it was a pity to see them go in at all, but if they hadn't, then the great days wouldn't have happened, so Mags and Brendan accepted the frizzling up of time. A day was a day and you couldn't expect anything more from it. The children were born, looked lovely and began to turn out well.

But two years ago, steady work became a thing of history and Brendan's ease began to wobble. It was just at the time when the children seemed to be costing more, the mortgage had gone up, the house needed to be painted, some of the gutters needed repairing, Mags had to have her teeth done – if she didn't have them done now, they'd fall out – the school tours cost a fortune. Every second year half the classes in the school went on a major tour. Their children were all two years apart. If they hadn't planned so well the school tours wouldn't have cost so much. That year it was Chester, Paris and Russia. And somehow, between one thing and the other, that year became their lives, that year became nothing more than a scramble to the surface to gasp for air. They kept their mouths open as wide as possible when they breathed in. The Christmas presents, one bicycle, one computer, one musicmaker, finished them off completely.

The slither down to poverty has no music to go with it. It's not a thing that can be portrayed by a loud thunderous clang, a steady march, a mournful sonata. It is too un-obvious, it takes too long, it is too unpretty. Brendan began to make lists in his head and say them out loud. The lists nearly drove him mad. On good days they were about getting on with it. On bad days they were, well, bad. He would have done some work on the house but the list of what it would cost didn't balance the pros. Despite all this, some-times Mags and he folded into each other as if there were paid bills cramming every drawer in the house. Those times made the next day smell of spring, but it was always spring before winter.

Uinseann McGrath called at six o'clock one Wednesday to tell Brendan that there was two days' work on a job at the top of Rathmines. Finishing job, all the renovation gear is there and you'd never know, the builder might be good for more, he has work all over the place. Brendan went down to Rory to tell him that there was work in it for him too, mixing, but Rory said no thanks. 'That's a mug's game,' he said, 'working your arse off as if it was going to last. Not for me, Brendan, I've a sideline on now. Come to think of it, I could get you ready cash any time.' So Brendan gave the work to Joe Sweeney instead.

It wasn't a proper building site. There was no foreman with a sheepskin coat and the woman of the house was there. The day started, yes, before they had even started, she made them tea and gave them Kylemore jam doughnuts. She chatted to her husband across the table while they all ate together, the electrician, an eel of a man, and his docile helper, the labourers, one of them who wore uncouthness like an emblem, the plumber, sleazed to exhaustion, the roofer, who had a toothache. She talked about the day's work ahead – the board finish, the bonding, the skim beads, the twelve-foot lengths, the Wavin pipe and three-quarter-inch fittings, that new plastic piping and fascia board.

'Skim beads, you could never have enough of them,' Brendan said.

'Lead's your only man,' the roofer said by way of reply, worrying that she might see to Brendan's needs before his.

The woman talked as if the table was not sitting on the only part of the floor which was not a hole, as if there wasn't dust ground into every square inch around her, including the mugs and the teapot, as if there were windows in her house, as if there were walls and ceilings and doors, as if the bath wasn't sitting in the middle of the kitchen floor, gradually being broken, as passing tradesmen dropped tools on it, as if she and her husband would get over this some day.

Brendan started working. He was attended rhythmically, silently, by his helper. Joe Sweeney brought the right mixture with the right consistency at the right time. They were like dancers. Brendan plastered the walls, sprinkling them first. He twisted his wrist and threw as a man would sowing corn from a bag tied around his neck. He spread and plastered with lavish sweeping motions, rushing here and to that spot there, swiping unevenness off the face of the wall, tiptoeing then and brushing quietly, smoothing over the jaggedness as in the last waltz, before moving on to the next patch to start again. He loved working. He was still the best plasterer he'd ever met, he thought, he'd never forgotten a thing that was worth remembering about the job. He smelled the smell of building, funny how you notice things when you're not with them every day. One of the labourers, the quiet one, finished some tricky job and leaned over it admiringly, 'Handy as a wee cunt,' he said, and Brendan hoped that the woman didn't overhear, but he saw her smiling a private smile.

They had tuna, peeled tomatoes, lettuce, eggs, cheddar cheese and scallions mixed on brown bread for lunch. Brendan knew that the tomatoes were peeled because Mags had shown him what a difference that makes to the texture of the sandwich. Would the woman of the house keep up this standard right through the job?

150

He went back to work, appraising first what he had already done. He fitted the skim bead in one movement and ran his hand down over it. This was spring before summer. He was paid in cash that evening, the notes were like silk handkerchiefs between his fingers.

The following morning Mags said, 'It's Chris's birthday next week. Get him some small thing. Just some small anything. A crossword book maybe or some small thing.'

Brendan thought, for God's sake I have only two days' work. He could feel his fury breaking inside him. It started in his stomach, went up into a word that spattered into more words, it went into a sneer, it turned the volume up on his bile, it put music to his rage – now that's something that does have its own symphony – it screamed at her stupidity, it banged its flat hand on the table, bouncing dishes up and down. He swallowed and never said a word. It wasn't her fault. The swallow tasted of razor blades.

'Are you all right? You look pale,' Mags said.

'Grand, no I'm grand.' He went to work and because he was such a good plasterer he finished in one and three-quarter days instead of two. Less pay.

Brendan walked to the bus stop, he would get an 83 outside Hynes's. The guards used to drink in there when it was O'Byrne's. It was a furtive, smirched place then. He and Mags had drunk there sometimes when they were going out, if they couldn't get a seat in Slattery's or in the public bar in Madigan's. They wouldn't have been caught dead in the lounge in Madigan's. The Fine Gael Party met there, which was bad, but if they weren't there it was worse, because everyone could hear every word you said. There were guards in there too. Why should Brendan worry about guards? He had never broken the law in his life nor did he intend to.

The 83 struggled down Rathmines Road. Brendan slipped along with it, remembering when names of streets and pubs used to mean something definite to him. A change in roofs, a peculiar shape to a window or a glimpse of a side street, he used to notice these things. In George's Street he saw a shop's tactless boast – LIQUIDATION SHOP. CUSTOMERS WANTED. NO EXPERIENCE NECESSARY. He got off at the next stop, maybe he could get something for Chris there, something cheap that would have been dearer in better times. He waded through pots and pans, crockery, screwdrivers, hotwater bottles, getting dizzy. There wasn't a damn thing you could buy for a child. He came out and leaned against the litter bin; he had a stitch in his side and he had wasted a bus fare.

Now let's see that list again. Outgoings against incomings. Mortgage, dole. Bus fares, dribs and drabs from the EHB. Food, Children's Allowance. The phone was gone. They hadn't had a car for three years, although Mags, always the optimist, kept the licence renewed. The three pound that Joe pays him back from that loan he gave him years ago. An odd drink, and how come it tastes better now than it had ever? one sip of the first and he wants a second. Once he's ordered the second he craves for a third. He had never been a big drinker. When it came to the third, one of the men would say, 'Brendan'll be goin' now, home to the missus, can't get enough of her.' Hey, Brendan. Hey, Brendan. Now, say if the mortgage went down and the

Children's Allowance went up and they did all their shopping at Crazy Prices in one swipe and he asked Joe for more than three pound towards the debt and say . . .

'Taking a rest Brendan?' Rory said, clapping him on the back, sending the pain scattering through him.

'Remember what you said about that sideline? Well, if anything comes up . . .' There. He'd said it.

'Certainly, Brendan, certainly.'

Rory called at his house a few weeks later. He was pale and jumpy. He wanted Brendan to do something urgently. Luckily Mags was out. A young fellow had taken a shot.

'I don't want to know nothing,' Brendan said.

'There's a few hundred in it for you. A good few. All you have to do is collect the doctor from James's Hospital. It's all arranged with her. You'll be given a car.'

'Right,' Brendan said.

Mags came back. He left with Rory in Rory's car. No problem with that – they were going to price a job.

Brendan kept his mind shut tight but tried to remember at the same time which streets they were going through. He would have to remember his way back, he would just have to. In the flat, two men plastered make-up on his face. It made him as inconspicuous as a lighthouse, but he had to believe that they knew what they were doing. When they brought him to the car, he doubted it. The back window was broken. It looked for all the world as if it had been stolen within the last hour. Dear God, please no. The bloody back window was broken. Steady, he said there's a few hundred pound in it. A good few. What's a few? What's a good few? Good was a word he was never sure of. He reached in and cleared the jagged pieces of glass, not daring to look over his shoulder.

He drove stiffly. The make-up on his face began to run down his neck, but he was afraid to wipe it away. A sliver of early March sun glaring through the windscreen wasn't helping. Only good thing about that, a sunny morning made the back window less noticeable. Two women crossed the road gesticulating to high heavens, he could imagine them taking off in one of those gestures. It was so ordinary, so secure, one of them put her hand on her heart, Mags does that and says honest to God at the same time. He had to slam on the brakes or he would have hit them. They turned faces ferociously to him and one of them puckered curiously. He sped away.

The doctor got into the back of the car nonchalantly. She sat behind him as if she did this every day of the week. It calmed Brendan down. There was nothing wrong with what he was doing, a work of mercy, never mind the money. I'm with the doctor, that would cover a person for anything. He hoped she wouldn't notice the make-up caking now behind his ears. He found the right block of flats, and the right hall and the right number. He tapped twice casually with the back of his hand. The man who had brought him to the car opened the door and let them in. He left Brendan standing in the hallway and brought the doctor into the kitchen. There was no sign of Rory. Brendan stood in the narrow hallway, stiff again with fear, listening to the doctor's quiet voice. How long would it take her? She was out again in what seemed like a minute.

'Are you done?' Brendan asked, smiling.

She looked at him with disappointment. She had thought he might have known better. Brendan flinched, mad with himself for letting his relief make him stupid.

'We'll go back to the hospital now to get what I need. Your friends have offered to get it in the Maternity Hospital – the Maternity Hospital, I ask you, seems they know someone there – but I think it's best if I try to get it.' She added, 'Don't you think?' because Brendan looked wounded.

'They're not my friends, I never met them before,' he said, and heard how silly that sounded.

'Well, whatever,' the doctor said, raising an eyebrow sceptically, 'back we go.'

Brendan hadn't bargained for this, running around the city all day in a probably stolen car. But there was nothing for it now. The doctor didn't speak on the way back. She appeared preoccupied. Is that window making her cold? he wondered. Obviously she was running a risk too, he thought.

'Park here,' she said when he reached the gate, and she got out quickly. Brendan put his hands to his head. Something inside it was thumping wildly. Let this day be over, but sense told him that fear would only drag it out. He pretended that he was an ordinary taxi driver. He looked around the car for something to rub the make-up off his face, the inside of his ear was tickling, some of it must have trickled into it, he must look an awful sight. The doctor came out again and almost skipped in beside him, settling herself in the front seat, holding a box on her knee.

'Well, so far, so good,' she said.

'Where to, madam?' he said, and she laughed.

He relaxed again. He liked driving, the same way he liked working. That show of sun was cheerful really, flashing light on walls that had been hidden by rain for months.

The doctor said, 'The one problem I fear is that it could be lodged very near the carotid. If that's the case, if I were to slip even one-eighth of an inch, we'd be in serious trouble . . .'

Brendan shivered and felt himself stiffen again.

'There's a hole on the right side, nasty looking, where the bullet went in. That can be protected with peroxide. But it's the other side that worries me. I think his bone is sore too, it went right through, it made the hole first and then went right through, hitting the bone along the way, I have no doubt. It's near the surface really, on the left side, half an inch down, that's all, I think. You can feel it if you press hard, although that's difficult because it's very painful for him.'

Brendan could feel his stomach heaving.

'I'll have to get them to agree that if anything goes wrong, if he does start to haemorrhage heavily, they will call an ambulance. Will you do that?'

'If you don't mind, doctor, I'll just do the driving first,' Brendan said. He was glad to have spoken because then he could swallow.

'Oh, you're not going pale on me,' she teased him.

He'd better pull himself together; if he had to stop to vomit on the side of the road, it would surely bring attention on them. If only she'd stop talking about it. Under his index finger, he could feel the bullet in the man's neck. The skin covering it was hot and purple, ready to burst. Jesus Christ, would this day ever be over?

The doctor helped him find the place this time. When he knocked, the same man came out and pulled the two of them into the kitchen quickly. He seemed more nervous this time. Either the man with the bullet was in worse pain or the strain of waiting here with all the curtains drawn was building up in him. There was the patient now, sitting on a chair, his face white as chalk, pulling at a cigarette, his eyes sunk into unmentioned pain. The others were crowded around him.

'Did you get the thing?' man number one said.

'Yes,' the doctor said authoritatively. 'Now, I'll need one of you with me and I think the rest of you should go into another room.'

'Righto,' the oldest man said, 'right.'

'Perhaps you'd like to stay with me?' she said to Brendan.

'Ah no,' he said, 'someone who knows him should be with him', thinking that up in a flash out of a reservoir of possible excuses.

The doctor smiled. 'True,' she said.

So the older man opted to stay. The other three and Brendan walked out through the narrow hall to a room opposite.

'What about the ambulance?' the doctor said, as they all tried to crowd through the door together.

'Oh yes.' Brendan stopped and the other three had to stop with him. 'The doctor says that if the man starts to bleed heavily, we'd – you'd – have to get an ambulance immediately.'

They looked at him, silently.

'She wants to stress' – now that's a great word, he thought – 'that if you don't promise to do that, then she can't start,' he added, of his own accord. In his heart of hearts he knew that if this went wrong he wouldn't see these four for lightning, it would be himself and the doctor who would get the man to the hospital. He would stand by her if the worst came to the worst.

'Whatever she says,' the older man said.

Brendan and the three men went into the room. It was empty except for two bare single beds. They sat on them, two to each. Brendan could smell the damp. At least some part of him was still functioning. The men listened intently for the first long minutes. They waited silently for either screams or police cars. When no sound came they lit up cigarettes and started to talk among themselves. They nodded to Brendan every now and again but made no serious attempt to include him, which was just as well, because he had by now set into a frozen lump. Two of the men talked about dog fights, the disgrace they were and more, the blood and guts of them and the cruelty. Brendan said a no-nonsense prayer. The third man suddenly said, 'Anyone want chips?' The other two said yes that was a good idea. 'Want chips?' he said to Brendan, just a little sneeringly.

'No thanks,' Brendan said, because much and all as he might have liked to please the man, chips were out of the question.

'And a batter burger for me, as well.'

One of them would drive.

'But what if you need the car to get to a phone? If you

need an ambulance . . . ? Brendan asked as if he hadn't already guessed.

They looked at him, taken aback, all three. 'Oh that, I'm sure we won't,' one of them said.

The doctor tilted the man's head to one side. She injected lignocaine into his neck and, having given it as much time as she could afford, she took out her scalpel. There was not even a millimetre of shaking in her hand. Inside there was a mild flutter, but that could have come from the challenge or the thrill of subterfuge. She told the older man to hold his friend's hand and to talk to him. He did so, closing his eyes and saying that all was going well and looked fine. She cut a perfectly straight line and gently prodded the bullet to the opening. She touched and probed raw flesh and bone; she felt the man go slack under her but she caught his head, let him pass beyond, and dug as far and as often as she needed until she plucked the lead out.

'There,' she said, delight in her voice, holding it in her forceps. 'Now your trouble is over.'

The man came to again and she fed him water. His face was now a transparent green and quiet tears ran down his cheeks.

'It is all right,' she said, squeezing his hand and thinking how lucky he – and she – was that she had missed the carotid. She talked to him, then, as she stitched, 'Don't move if you can help it at all.' And he didn't, but she could hear the little sobs coming from his throat. She finished that side. The other was blasted too much, so she would have to protect it as best she could.

'Now for the pain,' she said, patting him on the knee.

'Because I cannot get you to hospital, I will have to sterilise this hole beyond the call of duty.'

His fear began to dart about in shadows on his face, so she decided less talk, more speed. She told him to bear down and to grip the chair. She poured straight solution into his raw flesh. It bubbled like a boiling fizz and she had to say she'd rarely seen a man so brave. The rest was easy. She cleaned and swabbed and dressed. She wrote strict instructions for whoever, wherever, and told him how good he was indeed. He lit a cigarette and pulled on it as if the draw in could make an ordinary day out of this hour.

The doctor came out of the room exactly as the man arrived with the chips. The smell of vinegar met the smell of disinfectant.

'Would you like one?'

'No thank you all the same.'

Brendan and the doctor walked towards town. He was glad to see the end of that car. They were innocent now. At Bewley's in Westmoreland Street she asked him would he like a cup of coffee. He thanked her but said no, he'd better be getting home. They shook hands. As Brendan walked away Rory pulled in beside him. He had the envelope and he drove him home.

Brendan decided to introduce the money in small sums, at particularly bad moments. There is no doubt it would help, quite a lot. He relaxed into the only secret there had ever been between him and Mags.

Some weeks later, alone in the house, he was half-watching the six o'clock news. The reader reported that three men had been charged with armed robbery, Rory was named, and with attempted murder, following a recent shoot-out with gardaí. With WHAT? With WHAT?

'It is believed that a fourth man who may have sustained a gunshot wound was also involved. Gardaí are looking for witnesses and particularly call on any doctor or . . .'

Brendan didn't wait for the nine o'clock news to check. He left a note for Mags saying that he had suddenly got a few days' work around Dundalk and would be in touch the minute he got there. He packed the minimum, he did not want her to notice him seriously gone until the boat had well and truly docked in Liverpool.

When Mags got the letter, she borrowed the fare and arrived on the doorstep of number 52 Durning Street. She was there when Brendan came home from his job on the buildings. His mouth filled up with tears.

She said, 'Will you come home out of that?' She said that nothing might happen to him and if it did they could weather that better than they could weather never seeing him, because you can take one thing for sure, she wasn't coming here to live. He did come home out of that. Nothing did happen to him except that he developed a shiver up his back every time he passed Madigan's, or Hynes's, that used to be O'Byrne's.

TAKING SCARLET AS A REAL COLOUR
OR
AND ALSO, SUSAN...

I'll tell you what it says in books, Susan. I never wanted
to read and I wish I'd never started, but that's like an
alcoholic moaning about the Christmas pudding, it's too late
now. Not that reading kills you. Physically. I'm delighted
to be somewhere now. When people ask me, where were
you the day Bonner saved the goal? I can tell them without
shyness or shame. I know the exact spot, I was here in
Dublin, one of my sister's children was sick, so we were
watching it in the bedroom. We took turns putting our heads
under the covers; it was my turn, so I had my head under
the bedclothes during the actual second, I've seen the replay
though. The night the Americans bombed Baghdad I was
in a pub surrounded by citizens of the US of A. My luck,
it was the only pub in Dublin where there was even one
American. They were all there to hear the traditional music.
The musicians stopped and stared at the TV with the rest
of us, which was an odd thing to see, them doing the same
thing as the rest of us. We could have tried to pretend that
the sound of whizzing bombs was really a new-fangled syn-
thesiser backing a tune but it wouldn't have worked. Everyone was pale, except some of the Americans. There was no
more music that night. Susan, where were you? You go to
bed very early, don't you? The day the pope came I was
in Cork. Do you remember that? loads of people went to

Cork because it was a pope-free zone. Where were you, Susan? No, don't tell me, I can guess. But the reason I started to read was because I originally came from nowhere. When people ask you where you were the day Kennedy was shot, I bet you can tell them. Me? I was nowhere. Unless you'd call walking with my sister up on the ditch down our road to the shop, carrying a flashlamp that you had to shake all the time to get the battery to connect with whatever it's supposed to connect with, the frozen grass and weeds cutting patterns on our mucky wellingtons, somewhere. Which I don't. The band – the bagpipe band we called them as if we needed to differentiate between them and all the other bands that we had, or maybe we just liked the sound of bagpipe – was practising in Gladys Mahaffey's house, or, at least, it had been her house before she moved to the village. Gladys was a prostitute; oh, yes, there are prostitutes everywhere, even nowhere. She was a lovely woman, kind, but unwise. She had rakes of children, all of them she loved, Hickory Holler's Tramp wouldn't have been in it, the children looked like the shopkeepers, the farmers, the labourers, the van drivers. We liked walking on the ditch because when we were sent to the shop, particularly at night, my mother said, don't walk on the ditch, you might fall into the shuck. And we shone the light, when it worked, all over the sky, up and down from the tip of the earth to our wellington boots, dancing over the Milky Way, teasing it as we passed. It was probably the flashlight one of the band saw and then came out to tell us that President John F. Kennedy was shot. Killed stone dead. They must have had a wireless on all the time, which would be odd because you couldn't hear it over the drone of the practising bagpipers. It's more likely that one of them was late and had just arrived with the news. Or maybe they had known it for a long time and saw us and thought that by the look of us we didn't know Kennedy was dead and felt that they'd better tell us. We were from nowhere, so he could have been dead for hours and we wouldn't have known. Around that time I started to read to lift the aching embarrassment of being no one from nowhere. Gladys had some kind of fit one night when a customer was with her, a Mr MacM. The word spread, so the men stopped turning up, but it was great for Gladys because they kept paying her, to keep her mouth shut, so she always had enough money to rear their children. Look at some of the women in this joint, Susan, I'm surprised that woman's finger doesn't go blue or fall off with the size of that ring, it's as colossal as a street lamp. Susan dear, it's not true that I wouldn't say that if I was married, I have longed for many impossible things in my life but married has never been one of them. When I was young I would have liked to have had polio, I reckoned it didn't kill you and you could have an attractive limp. I would have liked any kind of limp really, I told you I was from nowhere. In the end I was expected to settle for a bookless life of drib drabs, oh but no, they had me sized up wrong. Here, do you want a light? did you know that every time you light a cigarette from a candle a sailor dies? I've sent shiploads perishing. I light a candle in the bathroom, put out the electricity and light a candle, very relaxing, and, of course, I've been to many expensive restaurants, where they always have candles. Some people would definitely say that I've done well, although I still think that a limp would have done me better, marked me out more clearly. But the books, Susan, I was talking about the books. I buried myself neck deep, I feasted, I swallowed, I took into me the way some people take vitamins. Imagine how I felt, I was somewhere. It was a long time later before it dawned on me that they were wrong about us. And that was a terrible thing. I still think of those books as the letters of a lover who turned out to be a fraud. What they didn't say about us is bad enough until you find out what they did say; yet, bad as that is, there is nothing worse than what they didn't say. A woman never had a baby in books, do you know that, Susan? Not once. There was an addition to a family, men ran up hospital stairs breathless to visit their wives who had just given them a child, there was a baby in the bed beside their wives where there hadn't been one before, or when a man died he had four children but a woman never had a child. There was none of that vomiting, no hysteria, no timid asking for him to support her back in the middle of the night, no ripping and tearing asunder, no screaming, no squelching around in blood, no enlarged vaginas. If we don't know what birth is like, we can conscript easier. That baby there, sucking milk, could become a war hero, Susan. So what? I say, anyone's ordinary boyfriend could become a hero, let's say, if next door went on fire and he rescued all the children or if he jumped into the Liffey to rescue an attempter of suicide – actually I don't think that's heroic, I think that's interference – but you know what I mean. You don't have to kill someone to be a hero. All the interesting things, Susan, what a fraud. And another thing . . .

stop getting your knickers in a knot, Susan, you're terribly easily embarrassed, aren't you? *And* you go to bed too early. No, I won't lower my voice, why should I? They never lower theirs. Come on, Susan, you remind me of a child I overheard yesterday saying to its mother, 'Mammy don't I have manners?' You have manners all right, where will they get you? We need to know things. Unmannerly things. What we need to know I'll tell you in a minute. If I wrote a book, I'm not saying I would, that should be a relief, oh, smile, Susan, a joke never killed you yet, all the same, Sister Brigitta, *an tSiúr* Brigitta, always said that I was good at English, she said it sadly, down in the bottom of her boots, because she believed that if a girl was good at English she couldn't be good at Irish. Poor Brigitta. I remember I liked the way words could bring you somewhere. I was very pleased to find out that 'hangar' meant a shed for housing aircraft. That meant that every time I thought of hangers, every time I tidied the room, every Sunday morning when I got my good coat out for mass, I travelled places on aircraft. At mass my soul was in a state of grace, which meant that the hole underneath my heart was now full of frogspawn, frogspawn was like sago, I preferred custard, mass would soon be over and we could have our dinner. Little things can be very important when you have to go to mass or when you're hungry. Do you know what I realised at mass one Sunday? I often said lists at mass, lists can pass the time, but I tried to say appropriate lists, the commandments, for instance. Susan, I found out that the commandments don't apply to us at all unless we're lesbians. Thou shall not covet thy neighbour's wife . . . See! And they're all

addressed to the same Thou, so! It changed my life, Susan,
I can tell you. Now, if I wrote a book, I'd like, on our behalf,
to admit a few things. I have slain my children, sent my sons
to war, peed in a cup in a guesthouse – mind you, I scalded
the cup in the morning in case people got germs – made
love with a dog, mind you, I put the dog down afterwards
in case it thought that people were for making love to. That
shocks you, Susan? well, they have pictures of people and
animals making love on temple and church walls all over
the world; of course, it's different in stone than in words,
you can blame stone easier. I did pray that my sons came
home from war even if they'd killed someone else's son and
I kept my mouth shut about the slain children, in case it
encouraged other women. No, I'd be OK. As long as I kept
the stories ridiculous, no one would believe me. If I wrote
that I jumped or flew over buildings as a means of getting
around, they'd say that I had a wonderful capacity to make
the fantastic real, but if I started my book by saying that I
had been blessed with two things in my life, an active imagination and a wet cunt, if you'd call that a blessing, now that
would be different, they'd say that everything in the book
must have happened to me, I couldn't possibly have dreamt
them up. Jump buildings and fly about all over the place,
grand, but the other! So you're right, Susan, I'd have to
be careful. There are people in books who take their
tragedies out to have a look at them, or they take their hearts
out to throw them away because of the trouble they've
caused. Me? I'd take the whole lot out just to have a peep
and if it turned into a gawk . . . well. Nothing wrong with
a genuine gawk as long as you don't start looking for

answers. Did you like History at school, Susan? did you like Parnell? I loved Parnell and Kitty, I would have loved to have done Michael Collins, I hated the Thirty Years War; anyway, I don't believe any of it any more, if they lied about the rest, I'm sure they lied about that too. I wouldn't write History, it's just selected bits of News, doesn't teach you anything unless you add it to other things, or at least the subject that they passed off on us as History didn't teach us anything. Where do they get the News? I hate the News. It's always about war or the possibility of war, or the aftermath of war. It's always to frighten us. If there wasn't any News, some of these men might behave themselves better. They drown us with News from places that have nothing to do with us, it gives them a way out of doing something about that funny-looking thing on their own doorsteps. They spend their time, these News gatherers, making sure that we don't enjoy ourselves. They depress us at night, and tomorrow, what does it matter? In the evenings in newspaper offices the mothers go home, followed soon after by the single women, who aren't that interested in war, really. The single men and the fathers stay on, the fathers, too, because when they were single men they always worked all night, so not working all night is not an issue for discussion. It's true, Susan, the bomb was always just about to be dropped, women lay in muck up to their tonsils because of it; then it wasn't going to happen, we were all about to go on an everlasting holiday, but no, next thing they're at it again. All those men up at night couldn't let it rest. Get them to bed, Susan, on their backs, I say, it's the only way to keep them out of doing us harm. Make them stick to recipes and patterns, that's what I say, Susan. I spent a night with a journalist once, had sex with him. I don't think he was able to take his mind off his work. I watched three seconds of him coming before I came myself. His eyes were open, he hung on for dear life, paralysed with pleasure, then he sailed away, hang-glided away, on the fright of it. Afterwards I sensed that he loved it but didn't like the intimacy of it. That's when I discovered how they get the News. They stay up all night, even after sex, because they've figured out that it's not night everywhere else. Later on, towards dawn, when a hurricane blew up in me again and needed melting, he said no, that he was busy, he had to write about how things affect the poor, that means the drop-outs, the mentally ill, the homeless, the unemployed. I asked him did he think that I didn't know who the poor are and did he really think that they'd tell him. I wouldn't, partly because I'd want to put my best side forward for him. Admitting the details of your poverty is not the most attractive thing on earth. Still, I must say, they do a good job, those men who stay up at night, so that people like me from nowhere will know nearly immediately that Kennedy was shot. Yet I'm not sure, who wants to know who's killing who when you're supposed to be dancing or asleep? No, I wouldn't write about History. In History we were taught about the famine and I agree we need to know but only if it teaches us that it didn't have to happen and never does, and we were taught that some of the Highlands were terribly badly cleared and we need to know that too, but what weren't we told? that's what I'd like to know, Susan. I used to read books to find out but I'm afraid there was nothing in them. Susan, do you think we're ordinary women? A man rang *The Late Late* one night and said that there were no ordinary women on the panel, he wanted an ordinary woman like his wife, but his wife's probably like us, Susan, and he doesn't know it. I think we're ordinary women, Susan, we weren't sexually abused as children, in fact I'd say our fathers pushed us away years too early just in case, it was nice standing there between their legs in the front of the hired car on our way to Granny's, of course, you probably got a bus, we had to hire a car to see Granny. I wasn't starved either, once, we had to eat porridge for our dinner, only once – I couldn't eat the bloody stuff even at breakfast time, it made me retch – mostly we had plenty of potatoes and cabbage. One day I suggested we have our dinner outside, our mother agreed, which is not a usual thing for mothers to do, agree to the extraordinary. I had got the old coats spread out in the garden, I had left the pan down, full with that beautiful fried cabbage and potato. I was on my way in to get forks, the dog ate the whole of it, must have been in three seconds flat. My ears can still sting at the thought of what followed. If I was an actor and needed to cry, I'd have no problem, I'd just think of the day the dog ate the dinner. As well, my mother made me come home from school early, the minute it was finished I had to come home, what for? I always asked myself. What for? It wasn't as if there was anything at home. People with good memories make good mothers. I'd never make my children come home from school early for nothing. But I am an ordinary woman, well, as ordinary as anyone can be, considering I was nowhere the night John F. was killed, and the lives

170

we've lived since and the lies we've been told. A person is only ordinary when they're slipping out of the womb and haven't been told anything yet. What did this man think an ordinary woman is? a woman who has read only a few books? a woman who has a few books but has never read any of them? a woman who has read the books that give her only the right words? for instance, I don't use the word foetus, I think I'm committing a sin if I do, I'm inciting to murder, as I said, Susan, stay quiet about the slaying. How could anyone be an ordinary woman; our mothers when they were children were sent out of rooms when a baby boy's nappy was being changed, Mother of Divine Jesus, it's no wonder some of us pick at penises as if they were going to bite us. Ordinary? Ordinary? How could there be such a thing, how could any woman ever give a guarantee that she won't go berserk some night and smash up the town? Which is why, Susan, I'm now going to change our drinks, I'm going to order champagne for us and tell you what I think we are that was never said in the books I read. First, the state of us, it varies so much there is no possibility of describing it, the picture makes no sense, so let's say, Susan, we are of such indeterminate sizes, measurements, proportions, that we are best left with names as a means of pointing us out. We are sometimes fat, thin, heavy-breasted, flat-chested, high-hipped, we are sometimes droopy with lust and drowsy with love, we are fast, we are tight, we are so loose the wind could blow a hole in our fannies. But the shape of us is not important. We love sex, we go wild for it at times, but you'd never guess by what they've said, now would you? We were stalking this country

171

in the nineteen fifties, early sixties, pleasuring ourselves and them, well, I know you and I weren't, Susan, only because it was before our time, but those lovely women, let's say, over in that corner, those women with the silver veins on their cheekbones, they were, but that's not what the books said. The books made us saints, cheap, plastic saints with lack of love or they called us scarlet, but they didn't see it as a real colour. No Irish book ever told me about love unless it was referring to carvings on church walls, back to the stone, Susan, it's safer. Do they think we wouldn't claw the earth for someone to turn to us at night and say, do you like it this way, sliding hands down around us, or that we wouldn't on a lonesome, not lonely, night turn to a body next to us and say, my place, there are a lot of Saturday nights to be got through? Or that we don't do it to ourselves? Crawl out of our single beds some mornings not fit to move? Do they think we only want what they've forced us to say is love, that we don't want a hand running up and down our clitoris as if trying to find it, a good warm breast that we can touch by putting our hands up a wide sleeve, that we don't want a finger with a grabbable wrist at the bottom of it, piff! one finger, three fingers, up our wombs, or maybe a man above, below, across us on a rainy night, determined to make us weak with wanting him? I ask you, Susan, how come the men who write don't know us? The men do. Look at him, Susan, no, not him, I don't like men with turned-up cuffs, not until I've spoken to them at least, the man beside him. I once thought that I'd write to Mr Miller. Mr Miller, to get straight to the point, you don't know your arse from your elbow, so to speak. It's not a door you're in bed

with, it's not a tight blank hole, it's not a gap – a gap is
only a between thing – it's not meat. Meat? You're fooling
yourself beyond the beyond. Not on purpose of course, it's
because you understand so little, you think you could eat
it; it's the other way about, Mr Miller. Although you'd never
say it, I'm sure that's what you fear and you have reason.
A cunt, not spoken to properly, could turn on you and
where would you be then? You caught halfway up and no
way of getting out, careful, Mr Miller, I say, careful. What
is wrong with you that you must do unto, ram, convince
yourself? Why are you so afraid of sex? Why must you
believe you have pulled a fast one? Why must you make
perversion out of passion and importance? That wild implor-
ing look, could you perhaps have read it wrong? I only ask.
Mr Miller, there are few of us who would not have cheered
you on if you had enjoyed yourself. And remembered
names. Were you simply looking for applause or trying to
get a reputation around town and were you perhaps an
erotic intimate under the candles? Mr Miller, why is it that
you cannot bear us to enjoy it as much, or even worse, more
than you? It is hard for you to know that sex is not forbid-
den to us. We have got permission and it's not from you,
it's from ourselves, all sorts, all shapes of us. The call boy
in you can pretend he's making the calls but your money's
running out. Now! Making love, Mr Miller, that's for grown-
ups, a creating of a shadow in someone's eyes, a passing
of the hand lightly over the down on someone's face, so
near to skin and yet not touching it. You know we do everything, we kiss across bottoms, we drive you mad with the
loss of your and our senses, we like it, Henry, although you

wish we didn't. Susan, I'd tell him about the things we've done; look at the things you've done, Susan, and no one would think it to look at you, no offence, Susan, you're beautiful, it's not that, it's the way you stand and the way you don't look at people, that's what would make people doubt. I'd tell him, Susan, that fucking isn't mere background noise to us. (Of course, I shouldn't single only Mr Miller out.) I'd tell him that I knew only one man ever who could make love properly and it wasn't him. This man, whom I knew, could make love by looking at me. On our first night, summer came in the dead of winter, the light coming through the window changed from watery black to red-yellow. In the restaurant afterwards we sat with our elbows on the table, eventually, leaning over, we matched our wrists, spread our hands together then joined our fingers. We would never be the same again, we were close enough to hurt each other by thinking. I should have been careful about that but how can you think when you're filling up with heartbeats? We made love all the time because that was the only word we had which seemed adequate to explain the torrential thing that happened to us, we couldn't get enough of each other, we drank our sweat, we to-ed and fro-ed, emptying one into the other, like children will when they play with jugs of water. We melted into a single body and sometimes couldn't figure out where one of us started and the other ended. His eyes filmed over when I came into a room. I could always see that, in the first second, before my own filmed so badly I could see almost nothing. I could feel my clothes on me all the time. As the months went on we got scared, I often put my hands around his wrists, my

174

thumb and middle finger would overlap because I have large hands. I did this deliberately because I thought it might bring me back to earth the way simple touches sometimes can. The bed we lay on – the floorboards many times because we couldn't always wait – took notes. I wonder did it ever warn me? I remember once in particular, this was before disappointment, we made love in his workroom, we could do it without a sound, if we had to, so the people beyond the four-inch partition would think we were reading or staring into each other's eyes at the most. We kissed quietly, touching our teeth, a voice that surely wasn't mine spoke to me, my blood made noise, he came high up into me as easily as you write Dear at the beginning of a letter, before you know what will happen. His phone rang, persistently, so he came out of me and walked across the room. His penis was covered with my blood, giving us all the comfort we needed. We had already bled into each other so this did not come as a surprise. As he spoke on the phone I came over him again and he turned inside me, making me a long warm shiver. He is gone now but that's another story. When I think of making love I think of his thumb held on my spine from inside, held there as a reminder, him smiling as if he didn't know what he was doing. I know where he was the night Kennedy was shot. That's the sort of thing I'd tell Mr Miller and he could show the letter to his buddies. Christ, there's my bloody landlord and I'm three weeks behind. Hello, Patrick, how are you? Come on, Susan, let's get out of here before he starts. Let's go to my place and read some books. Books you've never heard of, books we can grow up to. You don't have to go home yet, you can stay up

175

late for once. Of course I will, for you, Susan, anything. I suppose you're right, he wouldn't show the letter to his buddies. Still, you'd never know.

OTHER TITLES
from
BLACKSTAFF PRESS

I LOCK MY DOOR UPON MYSELF

•

JOYCE CAROL OATES

Whose story is *I Lock My Door Upon Myself* ? This novella chronicles the life of Edith Margaret Freilicht, born 1890 and called Calla by her mother who died giving birth to her. Elusive, wilful, eccentric, Calla is an enigma to the town of Shaheen, Eden County, New York, to her family, her husband, her children; a flame-haired beauty who views her surroundings and circumstances as a sleepwalker moving through a dream landscape. A woman whose life comes to be defined by her reckless association with a black itinerant water diviner, Tyrell Thompson. The fiction is told by Calla's granddaughter, in part to reach an understanding, a recognition: *Because we are linked by blood, and blood is memory without language.*

'possesses the same qualities as the painting that inspired it: beauty, strangeness and the capacity to disturb'

NEW YORK TIMES

'Oates powerfully creates a hallucinatory and harrowing atmosphere charged with sensuality and destruction.'

PUBLISHERS WEEKLY

'If the phrase "woman of letters" existed, she would be, foremost in this country, entitled to it.'

JOHN UPDIKE

PAPERBACK £6.95

210 X 140 MM 112PP

0 85640 474 8

THE FALLEN
AND OTHER STORIES

•

JOHN MacKENNA

The bitter grieving of a modern-day Magdalene; the sense-less, arbitrary death of a small boy; an otherwise decent rural community incited to sectarian violence by a bigoted priest; the slow blossoming of passionate tenderness between a man and a woman at a time of brutal war – human emotion at its most basic and elemental is the subject of this distinguished new collection of short stories and novellas.

Strongly plotted, starkly and beautifully written, they are an extraordinary blend of relentless honesty and profound compassion; with their publication, John MacKenna has moved into the front rank of today's Irish fiction writers.

'This is Mr MacKenna's first collection, but it shows him in full control of his content, technique and style. His prose is bare, pared down but most delicately shaped . . . it flows like a sliding, sun-dappled river. We'll hear from him again.'

VINCENT LAWRENCE, *SUNDAY PRESS*

'*The Fallen* is about people who thrash noisily about, unrestrainedly dramatic and obtrusive, refusing to collude in the weary calm of the defeated . . . MacKenna plays some narrative tricks that are as dazzling as the sun in your eyes . . . he is a very certain writer, and marvellously enriching.'

PENNY PERRICK, *SUNDAY TIMES*

PAPERBACK £6.95
210 X 140 MM 176PP
0 85640 495 0

A TIME TO SPEAK

•

HELEN LEWIS

15 March 1939: German troops enter Prague and for Czecho-slovakian Jews the terror begins. This is the story of one of the survivors.

'Helen Lewis survived the greatest nightmare ever dreamed by man. Her story is appalling, mesmerising, and one reads on with increasing gratitude for her clarity, honesty and cour-age. In these new and uncertain times, *A Time to Speak* is a cautionary tale of stark elegance.'

IAN MCEWAN

'It is a story of almost unbelievable suffering, but it is told in such a way as to leave the reader almost exhilarated . . . Her book is remarkable for its elegiac simplicity and lucidity, its irresistible momentum, its formidable integrity and its im-pressive lack of self-pity or rancour. It is short, approachable, gripping and patently honest . . . everybody should read it.'

SUE GAISFORD, *INDEPENDENT*

'Helen Lewis does not speculate, she never invents; there is only Truth, witnessed Truth . . . This book is the testimony of a woman who has survived the unsurvivable.'

JENNIFER JOHNSTON

'Rancid lies again besmirch Europe, and the lovely possibil-ities of cultural pluralism are being smothered. The world needs testimonies like Helen Lewis's . . . a book of utmost distinction.'

MICHAEL LONGLEY, *IRISH TIMES*

PAPERBACK £6.95

210 X 140 MM 144PP

0 85640 491 8

ORDERING BLACKSTAFF BOOKS

All Blackstaff Press books are available through bookshops. In the case of difficulty, however, orders can be made directly to the publisher. Indicate clearly the title and number of copies required and send order with your name and address to:

CASH SALES

**Blackstaff Press Limited
3 Galway Park
Dundonald
Belfast BT16 0AN
Northern Ireland**

Please enclose a remittance to the value of the cover price plus: £1.00 for the first book plus 60p per copy for each additional book ordered to cover postage and packing. Payment should be made in sterling by UK personal cheque, postal order, sterling draft or international money order, made payable to Blackstaff Press Limited.

Applicable only in the UK and Republic of Ireland
Full catalogue available on request